"Angus."

She breathed his name against his lips and felt hers whispered back. Just as they had always made love…silently. Nothing but their names confirming their identities, as if in kissing, touching, loving, they might lose themselves and need to know again just who they were.

His arms engulfed her, wrapping her in the security of his body, holding her close so all her doubts, fears and uncertainties were kept at bay. This, too, had always been the way. Safe in Angus's arms, she'd lost the insecurities that had plagued her all her life, living for the moment, living eventually for him and then for Bobby.

His lips were tracing kisses down her neck, then up again, resting where her pulse beat wildly and erratically. He found her mouth again, and claimed it in a kiss so deep it drew all the air from her lungs and left her gasping, clinging, wanting more than kisses.

Dear Reader,

Writing the CROCODILE CREEK series of books with three close friends has been one of the highlights of my writing life. Working out the overarching story, then sorting out who does what as far as their books are concerned, has been challenging, but it has also been an excuse for the four of us to get together—and as we live vast distances apart this isn't easy. This story is one of the final four in the twelve-book series and, in fact, is one of the four that are closest to our original concept, which was to set the whole series on a tropical resort island.

The idea of the holiday camp for children with ongoing medical problems, or physical or intellectual disabilities, is one that is close to my heart. In my life before I became a romance writer I worked with children with disabilities, providing respite care for them so their families could have a break. Working with those children and their families was such a rewarding experience, and they became so much a part of my life that they often infiltrate my stories, turning up as secondary characters quite regularly.

The CROCODILE CREEK series also became part of my life over the last few years, so it is with some sadness that I say goodbye to the town and its people, but I hope the memory of it and of them will linger on in the minds of my readers.

Happy reading,

Meredith Webber

CHILDREN'S DOCTOR, MEANT-TO-BE WIFE

Meredith Webber

HARLEQUIN®

TORONTO • NEW YORK • LONDON
AMSTERDAM • PARIS • SYDNEY • HAMBURG
STOCKHOLM • ATHENS • TOKYO • MILAN • MADRID
PRAGUE • WARSAW • BUDAPEST • AUCKLAND

ISBN-13: 978-0-373-06663-6
ISBN-10: 0-373-06663-5

CHILDREN'S DOCTOR, MEANT-TO-BE WIFE

First North American Publication 2008

This edition published by arrangement with Harlequin Books S.A.

www.eHarlequin.com

Printed in U.S.A.

CROCODILE CREEK: 24-HOUR RESCUE

A cutting-edge medical center.
Fully equipped for saving lives and loves!

Crocodile Creek's state-of-the-art medical center and rescue response unit is home to a team of expertly trained medical professionals.
These dedicated men and women face the challenges of life, love and medicine every day!

This month, sexy Angus Stuart comes face-to-face with the wife he thought he'd lost

Children's Doctor, Meant-To-Be Wife
by Meredith Webber

CHAPTER ONE

IT WAS, Beth decided as she helped other camp volunteers assemble the children for the night spotlighting tour in the rainforest, the best of all possible jobs. True, she was missing out on the gala evening that followed the official opening of the newly rebuilt and extended Wallaby Island Medical Centre, but to share the joy of a night drive in the rainforest with these kids meant so much more to her than dressing up and dancing.

With the extension of the Wallaby Island Medical Centre and the appointment of a permanent doctor—her very own self—to staff it, Crocodile Creek Kids' Camp had also been expanded, so now they could take up to twenty children at a time, providing a fun holiday with tons of different experiences for children who couldn't normally enjoy camp life. This week, the camp was playing host to children with respiratory problems and to a group of children in remission from cancer.

'No, Sam, I'll drive today with Ally in the front. You take care of Danny in the back. Remember he's not feeling very well so don't tease him.'

She settled the three children she was responsible for

this evening into one of the little electric carts that were the only mode of transport on the island, and guided the cart into line behind the slightly larger one that Pat, the ranger, would be driving. He had seven children on board with another volunteer, and he also had the spotlight.

Pat checked his passengers then wandered back to Beth's cart.

'You're a glutton for punishment, aren't you?' he said. 'Someone was telling me you'd just come off duty and you're volunteering for this job. Should be at the party, shouldn't you?'

He was just making conversation, Beth knew, but he was a nice guy and deserved an honest answer.

'I'm far happier out playing with the kids than partying,' she told him. 'And remember, this is an adventure for me, too. I haven't been in the rainforest at night.'

'Got your light?'

Beth held up the big torch he'd given her earlier.

'Now, your job is to shine it on the animal, so the kids see all of it. My light will hold the eyes and keep it still.'

'I think I can manage that,' Beth told him, although Sam was already asking if he could hold the torch and she knew they'd have a battle of wills about torch-holding before the evening finished. Sam might be slight for his eight years, but he had the fighting qualities of a wild tiger.

Pat returned to his cart and they drove off into the rainforest, taking the track that led to the resort on the other end of the island for about five minutes, before turning off towards the rugged mountain that stood sentinel over the rainforest.

The little carts rolled quietly along, the whirr of their

wheels the only sounds, then Pat stopped and doused his headlights, Beth pulling up behind him.

'Now, remember we have to be very quiet or the animals will run away,' Beth whispered to her charges as Pat turned on the big light and began to play it among the palms and ferns that crowded the side of the track.

'There,' he said quietly, and the children 'oohed' as the light picked up wide-open, yellow-green eyes. Beth shone her torch to the side of the eyes and nearly dropped the light. They were looking at a snake. A beautiful snake admittedly but still a snake.

Diamond patterns marked its skin, and though it was coiled around a tree branch, Beth guessed it had to be at least eight feet long.

She wasn't very good with snakes, so the torch shook in her hands while her feet lifted involuntarily off the floor of the cart. Ally, perhaps feeling the same atavistic fear, slid onto her knee.

Fortunately Pat's light moved on, finding now, fortunately on the other side of the track, a tiny sugar glider, its huge eyes wide in the light, its furry body still.

There followed a chorus of *'Ahh!'* and *'Look!'*

How could children keep quiet at the wonder of it, especially when the little animal suddenly moved its legs so the wing-like membrane between them spread and it glided like a bird from one branch to another?

Next the light was low, catching an earthbound animal, sitting up on its haunches as it chewed a nut.

'A white-tailed marsupial rat,' Pat said quietly, while Beth's torch picked out the animal's body and then the white tail.

The children's hushed voices startled the little animal, sending him scuttling into the undergrowth, so Pat changed lights, holding up another torch and shining ultra-violet light around until it picked up a huge, saucer-shaped fungus, the light making it glow with a ghostly phosphorescence so the children 'oohed' and 'ahhed' again in the wonder of it.

They moved on, Sam listing on his fingers how many animals he'd seen, soon needing Danny's fingers as well.

'You'll be onto toes before long,' Beth said to him, when Pat showed them the emerald-green eyes of a spider in his web.

'This is so exciting,' Sam whispered back. 'Isn't it, Danny?'

But Danny, Beth realised, was tiring quickly and, with a couple of children already in the hospital with some mystery illness, she decided she'd take him back to camp. Ally, too, had probably had enough.

'What if you go into Pat's cart and I take Ally and Danny back to camp?' she suggested to Sam.

'No, I'm Danny's friend so I'll stay with him.'

'I'll go with Pat,' Ally said, surprising Beth, although she knew she shouldn't be surprised by anything children did.

She shifted Ally into the bigger cart, found somewhere to turn her cart, then headed back, stopping when she heard any rustling in the bushes, letting Sam sit in the front so he could shine the torch around and spotlight the animal.

'Over there! I can hear a noise over there. Shine the torch, Sam,' Danny whispered, when they were close to the junction of the main track.

Beth eased her foot off the accelerator and Sam turned on the torch, finding not an animal or reptile but a human being.

A very tall human being.

A very familiar human being!

'A-A-Angus?'

His name came out as a stuttered question, and she stared at where he'd been but the torchlight had gone. Sam had taken one look at the figure, given a loud scream, flung the torch down into the well of the cart and darted away, heading along the track as fast as his little legs would carry him.

Danny began to cry, Beth yelled at Sam to stop, to wait, but it was Angus who responded first, taking off after the startled child, calling to him that it was all right.

Beth took Danny on her knee, assuring him everything was okay, driving awkwardly with the child between her and the wheel, hoping Sam would stay on the path, not head into the bushes.

'He got a fright,' she said to Danny, 'that's all. We'll find him soon.'

Fortunately, because Danny was becoming increasingly distressed, they did find him soon, sitting atop Angus's shoulders, shining Angus's torch.

'He's not a Yowie after all,' Sam announced, as the little cart stopped in front of the pair. 'I thought he was a Yowie for sure, didn't you, Danny?'

Danny agreed that he, too, had thought Angus was the mythical Australian bush creature, although Beth was willing to bet this was the first time Danny had heard the word.

As far as Beth was concerned, she'd been more afraid Angus was a ghost—some figment of her imagination conjured up in the darkness of the rainforest.

Yowies, she was sure, were ugly creatures, not tall, strong and undeniably handsome…

A ghost for sure, except that ghosts didn't chase and catch small boys.

Which reminded her…

'You shouldn't have run like that, Sam,' she chided gently as Angus lifted the child from his shoulders and settled him in the cart where he snuggled up against Beth and Danny. 'You could have been lost in the forest.'

'Nuh-uh,' Sam said, shaking his head vigorously. 'I stayed on the path—I wasn't going in the bushes. There are snakes in there.'

'And Yowies,' Danny offered, but he sounded so tired Beth knew she had to get him back to camp.

And she'd have to say something to Angus.

But what?

Not knowing—feeling jittery, her composure totally shaken—she let anger take control.

'I've no idea what you were doing, looming up out of the bushes like that,' she said crossly. 'You scared us all half to death.'

'Beth? Is that really you, Beth?'

He was bent over, peering past Sam towards her, and he sounded as flabbergasted as she felt.

'Who *is* that man?' Sam demanded, before she could assure Angus that it was her. 'And what was he doing in the bushes?'

Exactly what I'd like to know myself, Beth thought, but

her lips weren't working too well, or she couldn't get enough air through her larynx to speak, or something.

Fortunately Angus wasn't having any problems forming his speech.

'I'm Angus and I'm staying at the resort. Right now, I'm doing the same thing you're doing, looking at the animals at night. That's why I have my torch.'

He lifted it up, showing it again to Sam who took it and immediately turned it on and shone the light on Danny and Beth.

'Turn it off,' Beth said, finding her voice, mainly because the light had shown how pale Danny was. 'We've got to get back to camp.'

She wasn't sure who she'd said it to, the kids or Angus, but she knew she had to get away, not only because of her own fractured mental state but because Danny needed his bed.

She nodded at Angus—it seemed the least you could do with an ex-husband you found wandering in the rainforest at night—and put her foot on the accelerator.

They shot backwards along the track, Sam laughing uproariously, even Danny giggling.

'Little devil,' Beth muttered at Sam, turning the key he'd touched while they'd stopped to forward instead of reverse.

She accelerated again and this time moved decorously forward, passing Angus who was still standing by the track.

If the shock he was feeling was anything like the shock in her body, he might still be there in the morning.

Back at the camp, she left the two children with their

carers, explained that Ally had stayed with the larger group, then made her way to the medical centre.

Was she going there to avoid thinking about Angus?

She tried to consider it rationally, wanting to answer her silent question honestly.

Decided, in the end, she honestly wasn't. Little Robbie Henderson had been asleep when she'd come off duty and although Grace Blake was an excellent nurse and would page Beth if there was any change, she wanted to see for herself that he was resting peacefully.

And check on the other patients, of course.

And it *would* help her not think about Angus!

She parked the cart outside the medical centre, frowning at a dark shadow on the ground just off the edge of the parking area. A shearwater going into its burrow? She watched for a minute but the bird didn't move.

Hadn't Lily picked up a dead bird the other day?

And Ben, one of the rangers who was sick, had also been collecting dead birds.

'I was just going to page you.' Grace greeted Beth with this information as she walked into the hospital section of the medical centre. 'He slept quite well for an hour, then woke up agitated. Actually, I'm not sure he's even fully awake. Luke's here, but he's with Mr Woods, the man you admitted this afternoon with a suspect MI.'

Luke Bresciano was a doctor with the Crocodile Creek hospital and rescue service and, like all the Crocodile Creek staff, he did rostered duty at the medical centre. Officially he was the doctor on duty tonight, but Beth had admitted Robbie, talking to him about his family back home as she'd examined him, and the little boy had relaxed in her presence. If he was distressed, he might react better to her than to the other staff.

She went into the room where he tossed and turned feverishly on the bed, a small figure, his left leg and arm distorted by the cerebral palsy that had also affected his lungs, so even a mild infection could result in respiratory problems.

'Hey, Robbie!' she said quietly, sitting by the bed and taking his hand in hers, smoothing back his floppy dark hair from his forehead, talking quietly to him.

He opened his eyes and looked at her but she knew he wasn't seeing her, lost as he was in some strange world his illness had conjured up.

'Go to sleep,' she told him, gently smoothing his eyes shut with the palm of his hand. 'I'll stay with you, little man. I'll look after you.'

And holding his hand, she began to sing, very softly, a funny little song she remembered someone singing when she'd been very young, about an echo.

Had the song sprung from her subconscious as a result of seeing Angus—as a result of that echo from the past?

Surely not, but seeing Angus had unsettled her so she sang to calm herself as well as Robbie, changing to other songs, silly songs, singing quietly until the panicky feeling in her chest subsided and the peace she'd found on this island haven returned.

So what if Angus was here? She was over Angus. Well, if not over him, at least she'd managed to tuck him away into some far corner of her mind—like mementos tucked away in an attic. Could memories gather enough cobwebs to become invisible?

To be forgotten?

Not when they still caused pain in her heart.

'Bother Angus!' she muttered, then hurriedly checked that her words hadn't disturbed Robbie.

They hadn't, but what made her really angry was that the peace she'd found in this place—even in so short a time—could be so fragile that seeing Angus had disturbed it.

Here, working in a medical centre with a kids' camp attached, she'd thought she'd found the perfect job. Caring for the children, playing with them, sharing their experiences, she was finally getting over the loss of her own child—her and Angus's child. In the three years since Bobby had died and she and Angus had parted, this was the closest she'd come to finding happiness again. Ongoing happiness, not just moments or days of it.

At first she'd wondered how she'd cope with the kids, especially with the fact that many of the children at the camp had cerebral palsy, the condition Bobby had suffered from. But from the day of their arrival she'd known that didn't matter. Just as Bobby, young though he'd been, only three when he'd died, had fought against the limitations of his condition—severe paralysis—so these kids, whether asthmatics, diabetics, in remission from cancer or with CP, got on with their lives with cheerful determination, relishing every fun-filled moment of camp life, and drawing staff and volunteers into the joy with them.

Yes, it was the perfect job, in a perfect place—a tropical island paradise. What more could a woman want?

The L-word sneaked into her mind.

Pathetic, that's what she was!

Had it been seeing Angus that had prompted such a thought?

Of course it must be. Seeing Angus had raised all kinds of spectres, weird spectres considering Angus had never loved her—she'd known that from the start—although back then she *had* allowed herself to dream…

Not any more!

She pushed her thoughts back into the cobwebby attic. So what if he was on the island? He was at the resort at the other end, nowhere near the camp or medical centre, so there was no reason for them to meet again.

None!

Except that the island was no longer a haven, she admitted to herself in the early hours of the morning when Robbie slept but her own fears came to the fore, tiredness magnifying them.

She'd tried to tell herself she was unsettled because of the Angus incident—because of his escape from the attic of her mind—but, in fact, it was a combination of things that had her so uptight.

So desperately worried!

Seeing Angus had brought back memories of Bobby's death. Bobby had died of a massive chest infection they'd at first thought was simply flu.

With vulnerable children was there ever 'simple' flu?

And then there were the birds…

Her island paradise had become a place of sick children and dead birds!

The combination of words played again and again—like an echo—in Beth's head as day dawned, grey and wary, outside the window. Now, tired though she was, she tried to put aside emotion and just list the facts.

The celebration of the opening the previous day had been dampened by the fact that the ten-bed hospital attached to the medical centre was half-full. Sick adults were bad enough, but the sick children?

Lily, Jack and Robbie hospitalised here in the medical centre, Danny not well last night. For these children a simple cold was a big concern—flu was even worse.

Bird flu!

Not a fact but an inescapable thought…

The feared words hadn't yet been spoken but Beth imagined she could hear them murmuring on the soft tropical wind that blew across the island and whispering at her from the palm fronds. The worrying thing, as far as Beth could see, was that no one was doing anything to find out if this might be the flash point of a pandemic.

Charles Wetherby, head of Crocodile Creek Hospital and the prime mover in expanding the medical presence on Wallaby Island, would normally have taken charge, but he'd been distracted by the official events and the dignitaries attending them, to say nothing of the fact that his ward, Lily, was one of the sick children.

Distracted generally, it seemed to Beth, although she didn't know him well enough to be sure distracted wasn't part of his usual personality.

As far as the mystery illness was concerned, blood samples *had* been sent to the mainland for testing—that was a fact—but there were so many different strains of flu, would an ordinary pathology lab on the mainland think to consider bird flu or even have the facility to test for it?

In the pale dawn light Beth sighed, knowing she had to go through with a decision she'd made some time around midnight as she'd sat beside Robbie's bed, looking at the child but seeing a much smaller and younger child—not Robbie, but Bobby. *Later we'll call him Bob*, Angus had said, *it's more manly than Rob.*

But Bobby had never grown to be a man, and Angus?

She sighed again.

Angus was a short electric cart ride away, in the luxury resort on the southern end of the island.

Angus was a pathologist who specialised in epidemiology.

Angus would know about bird flu.

She had to go there.

She had to ask him.

Before another child got sick…

Before another child died…

Beth left the small electric cart in the parking lot at the edge of the resort.

'Stay!' she said firmly to Garf, the camp's goofy, golden, curly labradoodle, who considered riding in the carts the best fun in the world and had hurled himself in beside her before she'd left the clinic.

Garf smiled his goofy smile and lay down across the seat.

Not that he'd guard the cart for her—he'd be more likely to encourage someone to steal it so he could have another ride.

Smiling at remembered antics of the dog she'd grown so fond of, she walked along the path through the lush tropical greenery that screened the small cart park from the resort itself, and found herself by the pool. It looked a million miles long and she realised it had been designed to seem as if it was at one with the surrounding sea. At this end, there were chairs set around tables that sheltered under wide umbrellas, and closer to the pool low-slung loungers, where a few people were already soaking up the very early rays of the rising sun.

To her right, the resort hotel rose in terraced steps so in a way it repeated the shape of the rugged mountain beneath which it sheltered.

'Wow!'

The word escaped her, although she'd been determined not to be impressed by the magnificence of the newly rebuilt resort.

And possibly because she was so nervous over approaching Angus that she'd been concentrating on the setting to exclude Angus-thoughts from her mind, and talking to herself helped.

Then she remembered Robbie Henderson—and Jack and Lily and the other patients—and why she was there. With steady steps and a thundering heart, she made her way towards the building.

'You are not the wimpy twenty-five-year-old who fell for the first hazel-eyed specialist who looked your way—awed by someone in his position taking notice of a first-year resident,' she reminded herself, muttering under her breath to emphasise her thoughts. *'You're a mature, experienced woman now, a qualified ER doctor and head of the Wallaby Island Medical Centre. All you're doing is what any sensible medico would do—seeking advice from an expert.'*

Who happened to be the love of your life, an inner voice reminded her.

'Past tense!' she muttered at the voice, but it had been enough to slow her footsteps and she needed further verbal assurances to get her into the resort.

'What's more, he won't bite you. He'll want to help. In fact, it's probably only because he hasn't heard about the kids being sick that he hasn't already offered. And he's kind, he's always been kind—work-obsessed but, once distracted from his work, very kind...'

She'd been telling herself these things all night, repeating them over and over again to Garf on the fifteen-minute drive through the rainforest that separated the camp and clinic area from the hotel, but the repetition wasn't doing much to calm her inner agitation, which churned and twisted in her stomach until she felt physically sick.

'He's not answering the phone in his room, but if you go through to the Rainforest Retreat, he could be having breakfast there.'

The polite receptionist, having listened to Beth's explanation of who she was and whom she wanted, now pointed her in the direction of the Rainforest Retreat, a wide conservatory nestled into the rainforest at the back of the hotel building, huge potted palms and ferns making it hard to tell where the real forest ended and the man-made one began.

Beth paused on the threshold, at first in amazement at the spacious beauty of it and then to look around, peering between the palms, her eyes seeking a tall, dark-haired man whose sole focus, she knew from the past, would be his breakfast.

Whatever Angus did, he did with total concentration—yep, there he was, cutting his half-grapefruit into segments, carefully lifting the flesh, a segment at a time, to his mouth, chewing it while he attacked the next segment.

'The kitchens in hotels never get it cut right through,' he'd complained during their weekend honeymoon in a hotel in the city, and from then on it had been her mission in life—or one of them—to ensure his grapefruit segments *were* cut right through.

Although Angus's morning grapefruit hadn't been her concern for three years now—three long years…

She was trying to figure out if that made her sad or simply relieved when she saw his concentration falter—his forkful of grapefruit flesh hesitating between the bowl and his mouth. Which was when she realised he had company at the table—company that had been hidden from Beth's view by a palm frond but was now revealed to be a very attractive woman with long blond hair that swung like a curtain as she turned her head, hiding her perfect features for a moment before swinging back to reveal them again.

Reveal also a certain intimacy with the man who'd returned his concentration to his grapefruit.

Beth's courage failed and she stood rooted to the spot, wishing there was a palm frond in front of her so no one would see her, or guess at her inability to move.

But she was no longer an anxious first-year resident overawed in the presence of a specialist—she was a competent medical practitioner, and Robbie and the other children needed help.

Now!

Legs aching with reluctance, she forced herself forward, moving like a robot until she reached the table.

The blonde looked up first—way past attractive! Stunning!

If Beth's heart could have sunk further than her sandals, it would have.

'I'm sorry to interrupt,' she said quietly, finally detaching Angus's attention from his grapefruit, pleased to see he looked as surprised as she felt nervous.

'Beth?'

The word croaked out, though what emotion caused the hoarseness she couldn't guess.

'I'm sorry I couldn't talk to you properly last night but Danny, the little boy in the back, he wasn't well and I wanted to get him to bed. How are you, Angus?' she managed, blurting out the words while clutching her hands tightly in front of her so he wouldn't see them shaking.

He stared at her and she wondered if he'd written off her presence in the rainforest the previous evening as a bad dream.

His silent regard tightened her tension and she forgot about maturity and experience and bumbled into speech again.

'I really am sorry to interrupt, but we've a crisis at the medical centre and I—'

She saw from his blank expression that he didn't understand, just seconds before he echoed, 'Medical centre?'

'I thought you'd have heard—there was an official opening yesterday, a gala evening last night here at the hotel. The medical centre's at the other end of the island—an outpost of Crocodile Creek Hospital on the mainland.

There's always been a small centre here on the island but it was extended because after Cyclone Willie the Crocodile Creek Kids' Camp was rebuilt and expanded, and with the extensions to the resort it seemed sensible to have an efficient and permanent medical presence on the island.'

The words rattled off her tongue, her apprehension firing them at him like bullets from a gun.

'Crocodile Creek—that's Charles Wetherby's set-up—has a rescue service attached—yes, perhaps I did hear something,' Angus said, not needing to add, to Beth anyway, that if whatever he'd heard didn't directly concern him or his work then he'd have filed it away under miscellaneous and tucked it into a far corner of his brain.

But now he was frowning at her, the finely drawn dark brows above hazel eyes encroaching on each other, indenting a single frown line above his long, straight nose.

'And what has this to do with you?'

The question was too sharp and for the first time it occurred to Beth she should have phoned her ex-husband, not run here like a desperate kid, seeking his help. For a desperate kid was what she felt like now, not mature at all, standing in front of Angus like a child in front of the headmaster in his office at school.

Had this thought communicated itself to Angus that he suddenly stood up, pulled out another chair, and told Beth to sit?

In a very headmasterly voice!

But her knees were becoming so unreliable, what with the lack of sleep last night and the strain of seeing—and talking to—Angus again, that she obeyed without question.

At least now she could hide her hands in her lap and he wouldn't see them shaking.

Angus sat down again, pushed his nearly finished grapefruit half away and turned his attention to Beth. Most of his attention, that was. Part of it was focussed on pushing back memories and totally unnecessary observations like how tired she looked and the fact that she always looked smaller when she was tired, and she'd lost weight as well, he was willing to bet, and why, after three years, did his hands still want to touch her, to feel the silky softness of her skin, to peel her clothes off and—?

'Start with why you're here,' he began, hoping practicalities would help him regain control, not only of the situation but of his mind and body. 'Not here in this room right now, but on this island—connected to this medical centre.'

'I work there. I'm the permanent doctor at the centre. I saw the job advertised and thought it would be wonderful, just what I needed, something different.'

Far too much information! Admittedly she was flustered—wasn't he?—but…

He shuffled through his mental miscellaneous file—the Crocodile Creek Kids' Camp was for children with ongoing health problems or disabilities. Had she chosen to work in a place where she'd be seeing these children because of Bobby?

Of course that would be a factor, though it went deeper than that. On a resort island people—especially these kids—came and went. She wouldn't have to become too involved with any of them, and if she wasn't involved she wouldn't get hurt—Beth's self-protective instincts coming into full play—the same self-protective instincts that had made her adamant about not having another child…

Although maybe he'd suggested that too early—too soon after Bobby's death…

'Angus?'

The woman's voice—not Beth's, Sally's—made him wonder if he'd lingered too long in his thoughts. He was usually better than this—quick on the uptake, fast in decision-making, focussed…

He turned to his companion—tall, elegant, beautiful, clever Sally. She was relatively new on his staff, but they'd been dating occasionally and he'd suggested she attend the conference with him thinking…

He glanced towards Beth, weirdly ashamed at what he'd been thinking then furious with himself for the momentary guilt.

'Sorry, Sally, this is Beth, my ex-wife.'

'I'll leave you to catch up,' Sally said, in a voice that suggested any chance of them getting to know each other better over the weekend had faded fast.

But though he knew she wanted him to tell her to stay—to touch her on the arm as he said it—he made no move to stop her as she stood up with her coffee and raisin toast and moved through the room to another table on the far side, where other conference attendees were enjoying a far noisier breakfast.

'I'm sorry, I didn't mean to upset anyone,' Beth said. 'I'll explain quickly, then you can explain to…Sally? I'm sure she'll understand.'

The words made no sense at all to Angus, who failed to see why Beth should be concerned about Sally. Although Beth did have a habit of being concerned about everyone—even in little ways. He'd remembered that, with a twinge of regret, as he'd wrestled with his grapefruit.

'There's a bug going around on our side of the island that presents with flu-like symptoms but three of the children, Jack and Robbie from the kids' camp and Lily, Charles Wetherby's ward, are quite seriously sick, very high temperatures that we're having trouble controlling with drugs, and on top of that are the birds. There are dead birds, shearwaters I think they're called, all around the island.'

She glanced around and added, 'Probably not here—the groundspeople would clear them away—but over on our side. Lily picked one up and gave it to Charles, thinking he could cure it. We've vulnerable children in the camp, Angus, and although no one's saying anything, I'm sure in their heads they're whispering it might be bird flu.'

Her wide-set blue eyes looked pleadingly into his, asking the question she hadn't put into words.

Would he help?

As if she needed to ask—to plead! He felt a stab of annoyance at her, then remembered that Beth, who'd had so little, would never take anything for granted. And certainly not where he was concerned. Hadn't he accepted her decision that they should divorce and walked away without another word, burying himself in work, using his ability to focus totally on the problems it presented to blot out the pain, only realising later—too late—that he should have stayed, have argued, have—

But that was in the past and right now she needed help.

'Do you have transport?'

'Electric cart parked out the back.'

'Then let's go.'

He stood up and reached out to take her hand to help her stand—an automatic action until he saw her flinch away as if his touch might burn her. Pain he thought he'd conquered long ago washed through him.

How had they come to this, he and Beth?

CHAPTER TWO

SKIN prickling with awareness of Angus by her side, Beth led the way back to the cart, then sighed with relief when she saw Garf.

He could sit between them, they could talk about the dog and she wouldn't have to think of things to say.

'Good grief, what's that?'

Beth had to smile. Garf looked more like a tall sheep or a curly goat than a dog.

'That's Garf, he loves a ride. Move over, dog!'

Garf had sat up and yapped a welcoming hello. He was now regarding Angus with interest.

Was this a man who knew the exact place to scratch behind a dog's ear?

'He's a labradoodle, a non-allergenic kind of dog,' Beth replied. 'The kids love him and when they're all up and about he's usually with them. His other great love is riding in carts and it's impossible to tell him he's not wanted—he just leaps in.'

To her surprise, Angus and Garf took to each other like old friends, although Angus was firm about not wanting a thirty-odd-kilo dog sitting on his knee.

'He likes to hang his head out,' Beth explained apologetically, but Angus had already worked that, easing the dog to the outside of the seat and sliding across so his body was pressed against Beth's.

'I could make him run back—it's not far,' she said, thoroughly unnerved by the closeness.

'No, he's fine,' Angus said, so airily, she realised with regret, that he wasn't feeling any of the physical upheaval that was plucking at her nerves and raising goose-bumps on her skin. He might just as well have been sitting next to a statue.

A statue that kept thinking about a blonde called Sally.

'I'm sorry I interrupted your breakfast,' Beth said, and although she knew it was none of her business, she plunged on. 'You and Sally? You're a couple? That's good. I'm glad. I'm—'

'If you say I'm happy for you I'll probably get out and walk back to the resort!' Angus growled. 'For your information, Sally and I are work colleagues, nothing more. We're here for a conference. I'm giving a paper on Tuesday.'

'Oh!'

The relief she felt was so totally inappropriate she blustered on.

'But you're well. Busy as ever, I suppose?'

Angus turned and gave her a strange look then began to talk about the tiny finches that darted between the fronds of the tree ferns.

So, his personal life was off-limits as far as conversation went—Beth felt a momentary pang of sympathy for Sally who probably was quite interested in her boss and didn't realise just how detached from emotion Angus was. And personal issues like health and work had just been squashed; what did that leave?

Beth joined the bird conversation!

'The bird life's wonderful here,' she managed, her voice hoarse with the effort of keeping up what was very limp and totally meaningless chat.

'The night life's pretty surprising as well,' he said, ice cool, although he did offer a sardonic smile in case she hadn't caught his meaning.

'Well, it *was* last night,' she admitted with a laugh, remembering how strange she'd found it, in the past, that Angus, who was usually so serious, could always make her laugh. And with that memory—and the laugh—she relaxed.

Just a little.

'I nearly died to see a person standing there, then to find it was you.' She shook her head. 'Unbelievable.'

'But very handy, apparently,' he said, and she had to look at him again, to see if he was teasing her.

But this time his face was serious.

'Very handy,' she confirmed, although it wasn't handy for her heart, which was behaving very badly, bumping around in her chest as if it had come away from its moorings.

'How long have you been on the island?'

She glanced his way again and her chest ached at the familiarity of his profile—high forehead, strong straight nose, lips defined by a little raised edge that tempted fingers to run over it, and a chin that wasn't jutting exactly but definitely there. The kind of chin you'd choose not to argue with—that had been her first thought on seeing it.

Forget his chin and answer the question!

'Only a couple of weeks. I spent some time at the Crocodile Creek Hospital on the mainland, getting to know the staff there, as they—the doctors and the nurses—do rostered shifts at the clinic and, of course, the helicopter rescue and retrieval services the hospital runs are closely connected with the island.'

'Why here?' he asked, and she glanced towards him. Big mistake, for he'd turned in her direction and she met the same question in his dark-lashed eyes. Although that might have been her imagination! He had beautiful eyes, but if eyes were the windows of the soul, then she'd never been able to read Angus's soul, or his emotions, in them.

Except when he'd looked at Bobby. Then she'd seen the love—and the pain…

'It was somewhere different, a chance to see a new place, experience different medicine, meet new people.'

'Always high on your priority list,' Angus said dryly, but this time she refused to glance at him, keeping her eyes firmly fixed on the track in front of her.

'I've always liked meeting people,' she said quietly. 'I might not be the life and soul of a party, or need to be constantly surrounded by friends, but I enjoy the company of colleagues and patients—you know that, Angus.'

Did she sound hurt? Angus replayed her words—and the intonation—in his head and didn't think so. She was simply making a statement—putting him down, in fact, though she hadn't needed to do it because he'd regretted the words the instant they'd been out of his mouth.

For all her shyness, or perhaps because of it, she *was* good with people, knowing instinctively how to approach them, intuitively understanding their pain or weaknesses, easing her way into their confidence.

'And are you enjoying it? The island? The people?'

They were on a straight stretch of track, coming out of the thick rainforest into a more open but still treed area, and he could see cabins and huts nestled in private spaces between the trees.

Apparently more sure of the path now, she turned towards him before she answered, and her clear blue eyes—Bobby's eyes—met his.

'Oh, yes!' she said—no hesitation at all. 'Yes, I am.'

Then her brow creased and she sighed.

'Or I was until the kids starting getting sick. What shall we do, Angus, if it *is* bird flu?'

'Let's wait and see,' he said, touching her arm to reassure her.

Or possibly to see if her skin was really as soft as he remembered it…

He shook his head, disturbed that the strength of the attraction he felt towards Beth hadn't lessened in their years apart. Perhaps it was a good thing she had a problem at the medical centre—something he could get stuck into to divert his mind from memories of the past.

Although sick children were more than just a diversion—they were a real concern.

She pulled up in front of a new-looking building, the ramp at the front of it still trailing tattered streamers and limp balloons. The dog leapt out and began biting at the fluttering streamers, trying to tackle them into submission.

Was this the medical centre and these the remnants of the official opening celebrations? The building was certainly new, and built to merge into its surroundings—tropical architecture, with wide overhangs and floor-to-ceiling aluminium shutters to direct any stray breeze inside. Beautiful, in fact.

'Around the back,' Beth said, leading him down a path beside the building. 'The front part is Administration and a first-aid verging on ER room. The hospital section is behind it, here.'

They walked up another ramp and had barely reached the deck, when a woman with tousled curls and a freckled nose came out through a door, greeting Beth with obvious relief.

'Thank heavens you're back,' she said. 'I've called Charles, but you're the only one who can calm Robbie. He's babbling—hallucinating, I think—just when we thought he might have turned the corner.'

'I'll go right through,' Beth said, then, apparently remembering she'd brought him to this place, turned to Angus.

'Grace, this is Angus. Angus, Grace. He's the doctor I told you about, Grace. Could you take him around so he can see the other patients, introduce him to Emily if she's here and Charles when he arrives?'

The 'doctor' not 'ex-husband', Angus thought, feeling annoyed about the wording for no fathomable reason, though he did manage to greet the distracted nurse politely.

Beth hurried back to Robbie's room. The virus that had struck the camp had started off with drowsiness, and the children seemed almost to lapse into unconsciousness in between bouts of agitation. Right now Robbie was agitated, tossing and turning in his bed, muttering incoherently, his movements more violent than they'd been during the night.

Beth checked the drip running into his arm, then felt his forehead. Not feverish, she guessed, then picked up his chart to confirm it. The paracetamol she'd given him earlier must be working.

'Hush, love, it's all right, I'm here,' she whispered to the fretful little boy, holding his hands in one of hers and smoothing his dark hair back from his forehead with the other.

But even as he stilled at the sound of her voice, fear whispered in her heart. They were treating the symptoms the patients had without any idea if this was an aggressive cold or something far more sinister. Alex Vavunis, a paediatric neurosurgeon who was a guest on the island, had taken samples of spinal fluid from the sickest patients the previous day, but it was too early to expect results.

Beth knew her assurances could easily be empty—that everything might not be all right for Robbie.

'We've three children not feeling well, still in the camp, but Robbie and Jack are the most severely affected. My ward, Lily, was admitted yesterday and she's a little better today.'

Beth heard Charles's voice before she saw him, and turned to see he'd guided his wheelchair silently into the room, Angus seeming taller than ever as he stood beside the chair.

'How is he, Beth?'

Charles wheeled closer as he asked the question.

Beth shook her head.

'Agitated,' she said, 'although there is some good news. Jack seems a little better this morning. Lily?'

She heard Charles's sigh and knew the little girl must still be unstable.

'Jill has been with her most of the night. And Grace tells me you've been here all night. You should go home and rest.'

'I dozed between checking on the others,' Beth assured him. 'Emily's on duty today, but I'll stay now in case Angus needs some help with tests or information.'

She glanced towards the man who had moved to the chair beside Robbie's bed and was reading through the notes on his chart.

'You've how many sick?' Angus asked, looking at Charles who nodded to Beth to reply.

'We have the adult from the resort, one of the rangers and three children, making a total of five. There are another three children at the camp showing symptoms. We've moved those three to a cabin and the staff and volunteers there are entertaining them, keeping them as quiet as possible and making sure they take in plenty of fluids. Among the staff, the rangers, even people at the resort, there could be more who are simply not feeling well, people feeling the "beginning of flu" symptoms but who haven't said anything.'

'And you're how far off the mainland?'

This time Charles fielded Angus's question himself. 'A half-hour flight by helicopter—less by seaplane.'

'You've got to close the island, Charles,' Angus said. 'You must have had similar thoughts yourself, given the number of dead birds you say have been found. We have to quarantine the whole place—resort, national park, the camp and eco-resort—at least until we know more. It's a thousand to one chance it's anything sinister, but even that's too big a chance to take.'

Beth stared at him, sure her jaw had dropped in disbelief.

'You're serious? You think it *could* be bird flu?'

She looked at the little boy still twitching restlessly on the bed and pain washed through her.

'No!' she whispered, but she doubted whether the men heard her, Charles asking questions, Angus answering, Charles talking practicalities—how to enforce a quarantine, important people here for the opening who wouldn't like it, Health Department and Australian Quarantine Service concerns—

'It has to be complete and it has to start now!' Angus said in a voice Beth recognised as brooking no opposition. This was the focus Angus always brought to his work. 'It would be criminal of us to allow even one person who could be carrying a deadly virus to leave the island. And we'll have to get the police and health authorities to trace anyone who has left in the past week and to isolate those people as well.'

'That won't be hard. Most people here this week stayed on for the opening of the medical centre, and resort guests are usually here for a week, Sunday to Sunday. There'll be guests due to go today but not until later in the day. The helicopter pilots who do the passenger runs each day—they come and go more than anyone but rarely get out of their machines. Their manifests will tell us who's left so we'll have a list to give the authorities on the mainland.'

The two men had turned away, intent on putting their

quarantine order in place, as well they might be. It was going to be a complicated task, and more than a few people were going to be very annoyed about it.

Beth smiled to herself. Alex Vavunis, the self-important paediatric neurosurgeon, for one. He'd made life uncomfortable for several people, simply because he'd been upset to find his daughter, Stella, was growing up. Although being forced to stay longer might give him more time to spend with his daughter and to accept the new Stella—so good could come from bad.

And Nick Devlin, who'd stayed on longer than he'd intended already because his little boy, Josh, was enjoying the camp so much. But Josh was a brittle asthmatic and a lung infection of any kind could have serious consequences. Beth shivered at the thought of Josh picking up the infection, then felt a momentary pang of sympathy for Angus. He was the epidemiologist—he'd be the one coping with the fallout of the announcement.

Although Angus could handle that—work-related problems would never faze Angus. Only emotions could do that…

'We're definitely closing the island. Charles has been on to the quarantine people and the head of the state health department and she agrees it's the way to go in the short term but she doesn't want to go public with it and start a panic about a pandemic. Containing everyone on the island might help to keep the news off the front pages.'

Angus returned to Robbie's room alone, explaining this to her while standing in the doorway, his eyes taking in the small ward, and the child now lying quietly, seeming even smaller than he probably was because of the big hospital beds.

'In this day of e-mails and mobile phones, do you really think the news can be contained?' Beth asked. 'Besides, there were reporters and photographers here for the opening and though some went back on the last boat last night, I'm sure the local gossip columnist stayed on. Apparently she loves mixing with the rich and famous and the opportunity to spend time at the resort was too much for her to resist.'

Angus studied her for a moment and Beth could almost hear his brain working.

'Perhaps if we don't mention birds, just talk about a virus of unknown origin that has spread quickly, it might attract less interest from the press.'

'It won't work,' Beth told him. 'Most of the people on this side of the island know about the dead birds. And on top of that, you'll have to tell people to stay away from dead birds—maybe all birds—and the moment you say that, then the words "bird flu" will ricochet through everyone's mind.'

'You're right. We'll just have to ask them to keep quiet about it—maybe someone will have to speak directly to the local columnist. Explain we don't want to start a nationwide panic.'

'Or maybe we'll get lucky and some film star or other celebrity will do something dreadful that grabs the headlines and the quarantine of the island will go unnoticed,' Beth suggested, and Angus shrugged.

'Could we be that lucky?' he said, then he smiled and Beth felt a surge of emotion in her chest—a too-familiar reaction to an Angus smile. And just when she'd been doing so well—playing the part of the mature professional to perfection, though being in the vicinity of Angus was reminding her nerve endings of how good things had once been.

Physically…

'Charles tells me you're off duty, but he wants all available hospital staff, as well as hotel personnel, park rangers and eco-lodge management people, at a meeting in the lecture theatre at the convention centre at the hotel. Can you drive me back there?'

Beth hesitated, desperately seeking an excuse to say no. Even before the surge she'd known that the less time she spent with Angus the better off she'd be. But she'd asked for his help…

He'd come right into the room now, and stood beside her, looking down at Robbie, who was sleeping more peacefully now.

'You go, I'll keep a special eye on him.'

Grace must have followed Angus in, for there she was, flapping her hands at Beth as if shooing chooks.

She had no choice, standing up slowly, careful not to look at Angus, though every cell in her body was aware of his presence.

'Do you think it *is* bird flu?' she asked, and didn't need to hear Angus sigh to know what a stupid question it had been. 'Of course you don't know,' she answered for him. 'It's just that it's been in the forefront of my mind all night. H5N1, a seemingly innocuous grouping of letters and numbers, yet with the ability to make anyone who understands them very anxious.'

'From doctors up to heads of governments,' Angus confirmed, his voice deep with the gravity of the situation. 'But what we can't do is panic—or even become overly dramatic about it. There's a set routine for any disease outbreak—identify its existence, which we do by seeing how many people are affected—'

'Five in hospital, three segregated in the camp, and who knows how many who haven't sought medical attention.'

'Enough to cause concern in a relatively small population,' Angus agreed as they reached the cart Beth had used earlier. 'The next step is to verify the diagnosis.'

He sounded worried and she looked at him and saw the frown between his eyebrows once again.

'Problems with that?'

'Of course,' he said, climbing into the driving seat without consultation, but this was hardly the time to be arguing over who should drive. 'There is now a fast and definitive test for H5N1, a gene chip known as the MChip, but it's only been used in laboratories in the US. Out here we still use the FluChip, which is based on three influenza genes. It provides information about the type of virus but the lab then needs to run more tests to get the virus subtype—to identify H5N1, for example.'

'Clear as mud!' Beth muttered, although in the past she'd always enjoyed the way Angus had discussed his thoughts and explained things to her.

Or was it because of that past enjoyment—and the risk of enjoying it now—that she was feeling so narky?

'I'm saying tests take time,' Angus added, turning towards her so she saw his frown had deepened.

'I know,' she admitted. 'I must be more tired than I realised. Have you and Charles talked further than quarantine?'

Was she interested or just making conversation? Angus wondered.

Once, he'd have known—once, he'd have been sure it was interest, because that was Beth, always keen to learn.

Or had she been?

Had her interest been feigned because she'd known how much he'd enjoyed talking over his work with her? Discussing her work, too, until she'd taken maternity leave, then, with Bobby's diagnosis of cerebral palsy, hadn't worked after that, staying home to care for their fragile, crippled little son.

While he had lost himself in work, trying to dispel the fear love brought with it by focussing on genetic mutations of the flu virus—or had it been HIV at that stage? He could no longer remember, just knew he'd used work to escape the pain of seeing Bobby fight for every breath he'd taken.

Not all the time, not when Bobby had been well, and laughing with glee at silly things—but often enough, when things had got too tough…

He pushed the memories away—though not too far away—and turned to Beth.

'Was it hard, getting back into the swing of things at work?'

The question followed so closely on his thoughts he was surprised when she looked startled.

And puzzled.

'I was back at work before we parted, Angus,' she reminded him, and he had to smile, though it wasn't a joyous expression.

'You were putting on sensible working clothes and going to the hospital, and no doubt doing a very efficient job, but it was something to do, somewhere to go, somewhere to escape the emptiness—not something to enjoy or feel involved in.'

He stopped the cart and was about to get out, when he realised she hadn't answered him—not only hadn't answered, but was sitting staring at him as if he'd suddenly morphed into an alien.

'How do you know that?' she demanded, so obviously puzzled he felt pain shaft through him—pain that they could have lived such separate lives, that they had lost each other so completely in the thick emotional fog that had descended after Bobby's death.

Anger rescued him, blazing along the path the pain had seared.

'Do you think I didn't do the same? Didn't feel pushed so far off track by Bobby's loss that I wondered if I'd ever find my way back again?'

His anger eased as he watched the colour fade from her face and saw her ashen lips move.

'You never said,' she whispered. 'You never said…'

'We never talked it through, did we?' He spoke more gently now, shocked that she'd lost colour so easily. 'Not about the things that mattered. I don't suppose that's surprising, given we were two people who had grown up not talking about emotions.'

He reached out and touched her cheek.

'That made it very hard.'

He walked away before she could respond. Beth's eyes were on his broad back as she followed him towards the hotel building. He was there for a conference, he would know where the convention area was, and the lecture theatre.

But her thoughts were far from the upcoming meeting.

How could she not have known how he'd felt?

He'd loved Bobby—she'd known that much—and had grieved after his death, but that Angus had been as lost as she had been, *that* was the revelation.

'*You never said,*' she whispered again, this time to herself, but even as she said it, she realised how stupid it was to be surprised. Angus was right. They had *never* talked about their emotions. After meeting Angus's father, the only family he had, she had understood why he couldn't. His father was an academic and conversation in the Stuart family ranged over many and varied topics—scientific, political, even religious, but never, ever emotional.

In fact, going to visit had always been an ordeal for Beth as the cool—no, cold—atmosphere of the house and her detached, unemotional father-in-law had intimidated her to such an extent she'd rarely said a word, while taking Bobby for a visit had always made her feel inadequate. Dr Stuart Senior had produced one perfect child, Angus, while Beth had produced one small boy, who through an accidental loss of oxygen to his brain during his birth, had been, in the eyes of those who hadn't known and loved him, less than perfect.

Angus had stopped by the steps leading into the hotel and she caught up with him, looking up into his face, wanting to apologise, though for exactly what—not knowing how he'd felt, Bobby's birth trauma, getting pregnant in the first place—she wasn't certain.

Not that she could have apologised anyway. The look

on his face was enough to freeze any words she might have said—freeze them on her tongue.

'This way.'

Her heart ached at his remoteness, which was stupid considering they'd been apart for three long years. Why wouldn't he be remote?

And wasn't remote part of Angus anyway? He might have been one of the best-looking men in the hospital—not to mention one of the sexiest—but one look from his eyes, one tilt of his head, and even the most desperate of women would back away.

Which, of course, had been part of his allure to every single woman on the staff, and probably a lot of the married ones as well…

Angus led the way through the lobby towards the wing that housed the convention area. He and Beth had been together less than an hour and already he—or they—had managed to put up impenetrable barriers between them.

Yet seeing her had thawed parts of him he'd thought frozen for all time…

Seeing her had heated other parts of him—parts the beautiful Sally had barely stirred…

How could it be? He looked down at the shiny hair capping Beth's head, feeling a certain contentment just to be near her, yet not understanding why he should feel that way.

Familiarity, that's all it was, he tried to tell himself, but he didn't believe it for a minute.

No, there was chemistry between himself and Beth he'd never understood, no matter how hard or how often, in the past, he'd tried to analyse it. And it was probably, if he was honest, his inability to analyse it—to dissect it, understand it and so rationalise it—that had led to him allowing Beth to push him away when Bobby had died.

He'd told himself she was like a drug that wasn't good for him—that was the closest he could come to an explanation. And though he'd craved the drug, he'd gone, separated from her, telling himself it was for the best, pretending to himself he was doing it for Beth because she wanted it that way, losing himself and his grief in work…

'The lecture theatre's through here,' he said, touching her arm to guide her through a door at the end of the passage, touching her skin, Beth's skin…

Charles beckoned them forward, indicating seats at the front of the hall, taking his place behind a lectern, waiting for latecomers to find somewhere to sit, waiting for silence before telling all those assembled that the island was now in quarantine.

CHAPTER THREE

BETH watched Angus as he spoke, introduced by Charles as an epidemiology expert, explaining the necessity for quarantine until the source of the virus had been isolated.

Someone at the back immediately asked if it was connected to the dead birds, and Angus gave Beth a slight nod as if in confirmation of her words earlier.

'It is highly unlikely to be bird flu,' he said. 'But because it is similar to a flu virus, we believe flu vaccine might stave off infection in people not already infected. A number of you are hospital staff or are in related medical fields so have already had flu shots for this year, but we are flying in more stocks and will vaccinate everyone on the island who isn't already covered. This will be a big task but, like any task, it can be broken down into sizeable chunks.'

Hands shot up in the air as people wanted to question Angus, but Charles broke in to ask those with questions to wait until Angus had finished speaking, then, if he hadn't covered all aspects, to ask questions then.

He waved his hand to indicate Angus could again take the floor.

'So, vaccination programmes will begin, testing is ongoing and we should get results within forty-eight hours, but in the meantime we must act as if bird flu is a possibility, however remote. We know that more than ninety-nine per cent of bird-flu cases have come from direct contact with infected birds. So it is imperative we warn guests and staff to keep away from all birds, whether alive or dead. We have already ordered full body suits with rebreathing masks to be flown to the island. As soon as they arrive, the rangers will all be rostered on duty to collect and dispose of any dead birds safely.'

He didn't say that the cull might include all birds, not just the sick ones, but Beth suspected that would be the case and her heart ached, for the abundant bird life—the constant chatter and cries of the birds—was part of the magic of the island. She was wondering how it could be done humanely, when an irritated voice broke into her thoughts.

'You tell people not to touch birds. If we were allowed to leave—if everyone was evacuated—there'd be no need to worry. Why can't everyone who isn't sick leave now? We're capable of watching our health, looking for symptoms and getting to our own doctor if we should feel ill. There's no need for all of us to be part of this crisis.'

Beth didn't know the man who was complaining—perhaps he was one of the hotel management people—and she could understand his concern. The tide of dissent was rising, people muttering and mumbling behind her, agreeing with the man.

'There *is* no crisis,' Angus replied, his quiet, measured voice contrasting with the loud, bullying tones of the guest.

'The quarantine is purely precautionary. We are isolating the people who are already sick and those who are showing slight symptoms. The fact that the illness struck so quickly makes it likely that the quarantine period will be relatively short. The normal process is to isolate a community for a set number of days after the last person becomes ill. In the meantime, if you wish to remain isolated from other people, that is up to you, and I'm sure the resort staff will help you facilitate it.'

Would the man accept this common-sense explanation? Beth turned towards him and saw him take his seat, although his lips were moving and she knew he was muttering at the people around him, no doubt still complaining, while around him rose a mumbling of rebellion that could easily slip out of control.

'Excuse me!' The man's voice silenced the pocket of conversation. 'You're talking about vaccinations for those who haven't had a flu shot this year and saying those who have had one should be all right, but aren't flu shots virus-specific?'

It was Mike Poulos, a paramedic helicopter pilot from Crocodile Creek, who asked the question, and the practicality of it didn't mask the concern in his voice.

Was his concern for his wife, Emily, the doctor now on duty at the medical centre? Of course it would be—Emily and Mike were not long married and so devoted to each other it always warmed Beth to see them together.

'They are developed each year for the specific virus experts predict will hit our shores, but viruses mutate so quickly that by the time the Australian flu season starts it is usually not the virus for which the vaccine was developed. But the vaccination will help prevent other flu strains, and in this case having some protection could be better than none.'

Angus spoke quietly but the undeniable authority in his voice quietened the muted whispers and Beth saw many people nodding in agreement.

Was it because he was aware he now had the full attention of his audience that he continued?

'But remember,' he said, 'that we're by no means certain it is bird flu or, indeed, any other type of flu. The vaccinations are purely precautionary and are not even compulsory. We shall make the vaccine available to anyone who wants it, and Charles will provide staff to administer it.'

Someone asked a question and as Angus turned his head to answer, Beth studied him, trying to see him dispassionately—as a doctor and an expert, not an ex-husband. It wasn't only his voice that suggested confidence and authority but his bearing—his whole demeanour.

And once again she wondered what on earth such a man had ever seen in a little snip of a thing like her—a fellow doctor, sure, but when they'd met she'd been a first-year resident—dust beneath the feet of most men like Angus, men who were already making their mark and heading inevitably towards the top of their chosen fields.

Sexual attraction, that was the only explanation—some chemical reaction between them, something neither of them had control over.

It was where it had led that had caused the problem.

Familiar guilt weighed heavily in her heart—guilt she

knew it was stupid to feel as her falling pregnant had been a two-way street.

And Angus hadn't *had* to marry her—she'd told him that.

Except, being Angus and with very clear views on responsibility, he had insisted.

He'd married her because of her pregnancy, not because he'd loved her—that was the part that hurt.

She pushed the past away, worried that it still had the power to affect her physically, and tried to concentrate on what was going on in the present.

'Programmes for vaccinations. Any of you who haven't had flu vaccine please put your name and cabin or room number on a sheet of paper here at the front of the room before you leave and we'll contact you regarding a time for the vaccination.'

Charles was talking again, adding that hotel staff and guests would be seen at the hotel, while those in eco-cabins and the camp could come to the medical centre.

'And what if it's not bird flu?' someone asked, and Charles nodded his willingness to take the question.

'Well, you'll all be inoculated against flu for the next season's outbreak,' he said, smiling reassuringly, although Beth knew he must be worried sick about both Lily and the situation. 'Seriously, though,' he added, 'we are looking into that. We've sent specimens to the mainland and should have some information back tomorrow, or the following day at the latest.'

More questions followed but in the end Charles called a halt, telling everyone they'd be kept informed with daily bulletins.

Was it chance that Beth found Angus by her side as she walked out of the hotel?

Surely it was. And why was he walking out anyway? Simply to upset her equilibrium, not to mention her nerve endings?

'Haven't you a conference session to attend?' she asked, as he accompanied her down the steps and turned towards the cart park.

'I'm giving a paper on Tuesday, I can't avoid that, but I can get notes for the rest of it.'

'But going to the sessions would be better than notes. I know I asked you to help but that was mainly because I was worried that it might be bird flu and you'd know what to do about quarantine and things—who to contact. It's not as if we're short of doctors. Half the staff of the Crocodile Creek hospital came over for the official opening and they're all stuck here with everyone else.'

Had she sounded a little hysterical that Angus had stopped walking and turned to look down into her face?

'Is that a practical protest or a personal one, Beth?' he asked, not smiling but not frowning either. 'Do you really believe I have nothing to offer over there, or is it that you don't want me around on your part of the island?'

She stared at him for a moment. Put like that, her comment seemed remarkably petty.

'I feel awkward,' she replied, opting for honesty. 'It was hard enough coming over here to ask for your help, Angus, and now—well, I don't know the "and now" part…'

She walked on, getting to the cart and climbing in—behind the wheel.

'I wouldn't think we'd have to see much of each other,'

he said, apparently unaffected by either her actions or her words. He simply took the passenger seat and kept talking. 'From what Charles said, you're off duty for a few days now, and even if you're called back to help with the vaccination programme, our paths don't need to cross.'

It's what you want, she told herself, starting the cart and turning it back along the road through the rainforest.

Liar!

What you really want is to be near him again, for whatever reason, and that is *not* mature. In fact, that is pathetic!

She stared fixedly at the road ahead, although the little cart moved so slowly a glance now and then would have sufficed. But because her attention was so focussed she didn't know he'd raised his arm until his fingers touched her cheek.

'Are you feeling all right yourself? No flu symptoms? You're very pale.'

Touch me again, her heart shouted, beating so loudly she was surprised he didn't hear it.

'I'm fine,' she assured him, still not looking at him, afraid now he'd see her reaction—the attraction that still fired all her senses—in her eyes.

'Well, you don't look fine. That little boy who was hallucinating—did you sit with him last night?'

Lie?

How could she?

She nodded.

'Because he looks like Bobby?'

She stopped the cart and turned to face him, then a demanding beep from the cart behind reminded her that most of the medical centre staff had been at the resort and were now returning to their side of the island.

Started up again, staring ahead as she answered.

'He does remind me of Bobby, but I spent the night with him because he's one of a number of children who came to the camp on his own. Part of the reason for the camp is to give the family respite from caring for a child with special needs. Give the parents time to do things with their other kids—things that are sometimes awkward when one child is in a wheelchair or can't go to places with flashing lights. Anyway, when Miranda, the respiratory physician who's in charge of the kids with lung problems, phoned his mother to tell her Robbie was sick, she was distraught, because she's a single mother with four other kids and it's impossible for her to get up here.'

'So you offered to be the replacement mum.'

Something in the way he said it—not sarcastically, but knowingly somehow—reminded Beth that even when she'd loved him most, he'd still been able to infuriate her.

'You've got a problem with that?' she snapped. 'Going to give me a lecture about keeping a professional distance between myself and my patients? Some worldly wisdom about not getting too involved?'

She heard him sigh and glanced his way, catching a look—surely not misery?—on his face.

'Would you listen?'

His voice was soft—gentle—and it coiled itself inside her, squeezing her lungs and winding around her heart, snaring her so effortlessly in the net that was her love for Angus.

'No!' she snapped again, because she didn't want to believe he could still do this to her—or admit it to herself if he could. 'And for your information, if I've bonded especially with any of the kids it's not with Robbie but with Sam—the little boy who ran away from the cart last night. He's the cheekiest little devil, in remission for the second time from acute lymphoblastic leukaemia, but with so much fight in him that if anyone will beat it, he will.'

Then she sighed, relaxed, and smiled at her passenger.

'Actually, I love them all. I love being part of their lives, even if it's just for a short time. They're so grown up somehow, kids who've had bad things happen in their lives—so mature for their ages in some ways, but still little kids in other ways.'

'Softy!' Angus teased, touching her cheek with the pad of his thumb, tracing a line towards her jaw. 'Of course you love them all.'

The wandering thumb edged towards her lips, brushed them briefly, then moved away, leaving Beth a silent, heart-skittering mess.

How could Angus still reduce her to this state?

Did he know the effect he was having on her or was he just being Angus?

And how could she allow herself to be reduced to a helpless puddle of desire from one touch of his thumb?

Pathetic, that's what she was.

Hopeless!

The maturity she thought she'd found in three long years, gone with a smile and a touch of a thumb…

She pulled up at the medical centre, where people returning from the hotel had already gathered, awaiting orders from Charles. Mike Poulos was on the deck, looking anxious as he spoke to his wife, Emily.

'You have to tell Charles,' he was saying, loudly enough for anyone to hear. 'If he knew you were pregnant, he'd be the first to tell you to keep away from here.'

'Husband and wife?' Angus asked, and Beth nodded, although this was the first she'd heard of Emily being pregnant.

'Will you introduce me to them?'

The question was unexpected, but Beth could see no reason not to, so she led Angus up the ramp. Doctor Beth and colleague Angus—exactly how things should be! Though Angus's wanting to meet the pair seemed to indicate an interest in their problems—something the Angus she had known would have avoided at all costs. It was tantamount to emotional involvement—the very thing he'd been teasing *her* about just now.

And he *had* been teasing, not lecturing…

'Mike, you were at the meeting so you know who Angus is. Emily, this is Angus Stuart, he's a pathologist and epidemiologist. He's working with Charles on the quarantine.'

'Angus Stuart?' Emily said, raising an eyebrow at Beth.

'My ex-husband,' Beth managed, although the 'ex' part sliced into her throat like a razor. 'Angus, meet Mike and Emily Poulos.'

She stepped back as Angus moved closer to the couple.

'We couldn't help overhearing your conversation,' he said, 'and you're right to be concerned, Mike, but if by some million-to-one chance it is bird flu, it's unlikely that it would pass from human to human. There has only been one possible example worldwide where that *might* have happened. In all other proven cases it has come from contact with infected birds.'

'It's still a risk for Emily to be working here,' Mike

said, his stubborn Greek genes pushing him to protect his woman.

'Not if she's careful. All staff will be wearing masks and double-gloving, although gloves should never take the place of hand-washing. Looking at the symptoms the patients are showing, if it's more serious than bad flu, it's likely to be some kind of viral encephalitis, which is very serious and very dangerous itself, but again, although the underlying infections that cause it—mononucleosis, herpes, even measles—are contagious, the encephalitis isn't.'

Mike nodded but didn't look any less happy and Beth guessed he wouldn't be unless he could wrap Emily in cotton wool for her entire pregnancy.

'Dr Beth, Dr Beth!'

Beth turned at the cry and saw Cameron, one of the little boys in the cancer group, racing towards her.

'It's Danny, he's sick. On the track near Stella's cabin.'

Angus, Emily and Mike were forgotten. Pausing only to check that the cart they used for emergency trips had its first-aid box and emergency gear strapped on behind, Beth climbed behind the wheel and spun the cart in the direction of the beach. Garf came flying from nowhere and landed beside her as she moved off.

Susie, the hospital physio, over here for the camp, came racing up the path as Beth neared the junction.

'Seizure,' she said. 'He hasn't come out of it. Alex Vavunis is with him—said to check you had oxygen and diazepam on board.'

'I've both,' Beth assured her as Susie turned and trotted by the cart. 'Who was there when it happened? Is someone timing it?'

'Benita, the nurse in charge of that group, was with him. She called for help when he didn't come out of it. Alex and I were close by.'

'Alex is involved in paediatric neurology, isn't he?' Beth said, remembering talk about the man. 'Best person Danny could have around,' she added, when Susie nodded.

She saw the group and drove close, stopped, then brought the oxygen bottle and first-aid box from the cart to where the child lay. Alex slipped the mask over the child's nose and mouth and started oxygen, then, while Beth guessed Danny's weight—he was very small for six—and calculated how much drug he'd need, Alex slid a cannula into the child's vein, making an often difficult task seem simple. Once he was satisfied the line was secure and the drug was flowing into Danny's bloodstream, Alex glanced at Beth for the okay then lifted the child, Susie carrying the oxygen bottle and holding it while Alex settled into the cart, the limp child in his arms, the oxygen bottle placed between his legs.

Beth drove steadily back to the medical centre, where it seemed even more people had gathered. But she went straight to the ramp at the rear, so Alex could carry the little boy into the closest room, the one where Jack Havens was recovering from the mystery virus.

'You're not on duty,' Charles reminded her, as she emerged from the room after settling Danny into bed. He was wheeling towards the room, no doubt having heard of the emergency. Angus was beside him, the two men looking as if they'd already bonded in some way.

Both work-obsessed, Beth guessed.

'I've asked all the staff not on duty to leave the medical centre,' Charles told her. 'Keep your mobile phones or pagers handy as we'll be contacting you about rosters for the flu vaccine as soon as Jill and I have that sorted.'

He turned to Angus.

'You'll be around? I want to check out this child then get straight onto these rosters but once that's done I'd like to talk to you about further measures we should take.'

'I came straight from breakfast and don't have my mobile on me, but I'll walk Beth back to her cabin. You can contact me there.'

Beth opened her mouth to protest but as most of her mainland colleagues were still hovering around the bottom of the ramp, she shut it again.

Why had he said that? Angus wondered. He could just as easily have waited here, at the centre, maybe sat with the little boy whose mother couldn't come, but—

'I just want to check on Robbie before I leave,' Beth said, and although he'd been thinking of the child himself, and Beth had denied any special bond, Angus was still concerned by her connection to him.

She slipped away, but he followed, meeting a harassed-looking woman on the way.

'Jill Shaw,' she said, offering her hand as well as her name. 'Director of Nursing at the hospital over on the mainland. I gather you're Beth's ex-husband. Good of you to help out like this.'

Angus shrugged off her thanks, taking in the shadows beneath her grey-blue eyes, and the lines of worry creasing her face.

'I understand the little girl who is sick is related to you.'

'Related to Charles,' Jill said, twisting a ring on the third finger of her left hand—an opal ring, the stone shooting fire as she moved it. 'She's our ward—well, sort of.'

Jill was so obviously distressed, Angus touched her shoulder.

'It's hard, watching a child you love suffer,' he said quietly, and the soft eyes lifted to his face.

She saw something in it that seemed to settle her. She found a smile and touched his hand.

'It's more than hard,' she said, 'but thank you for your understanding.'

She whisked away, leaving Angus with the feeling that he hadn't quite understood the conversation, and doubting, for all her thanks, that he'd helped at all.

But Beth was coming out of Robbie's room, and he forgot the worries of a woman he'd just met to concentrate on his own concerns, the main one being that he could still feel such a strong attraction towards his ex-wife.

He watched her as she stopped to speak to a nurse, studying her, thinking, as he always had, how this woman had caused such havoc in his life.

It had been three years—surely he'd moved on. Surely—inner wry smile—he'd beaten the drug!

What he'd actually done had been to lose himself in work and though that was normal for him, for the past few years he'd pushed harder, worked longer hours, leaving himself little time for thoughts not connected to whatever project he had in hand.

Going to the US had helped, working in Atlanta's Centers for Disease Control and Prevention. It had been an opportunity granted to few, and he'd relished it—and worked even harder over there…

'He's sleeping, and peacefully,' the woman he'd been pondering about said calmly, smiling at him so the tiredness disappeared from her face and her eyes shone with simple pleasure.

Of course he still felt attracted to her, he excused himself, she was the most genuine person he had ever met, and that, added to an undeniably sexy body, was irresistible.

At least to him—

Or any man?

She was chattering on about Robbie and the other little boy, Jack, while Angus tortured himself over the possibility of there being another man in Beth's life. A man who might even now be waiting for her in her cabin.

Although surely she'd have said something—objected to his suggestion of waiting there.

'You don't have to walk back with me,' she announced, so perfectly on cue he immediately assumed there *was* a man.

Which, contrarily, made him determined to stick by her side. She was an innocent for all she'd been married. Any man could con her. His protective instincts went on full alert…

'I have to wait somewhere,' he said. 'And I'd like to see where you live.'

She slowed her pace and turned towards him.

'Why, Angus?'

Such a simple question but the equally simple answer—because he still cared about her—would sound ridiculous.

'Just to see,' he said, aware of how lame he sounded, but, tired though she must be, she smiled.

'It's not so different from the flat I had when we first

met,' she told him. 'The kind of place that will make you reel back in horror. Junk everywhere—not all mine, because some was already there—but I'm still a magpie and beachcombing yields such unlikely treasures I hate to part with any of them.'

They were walking along a narrow path, in the dense shade of the huge soft-wooded trees that grew among the palms and ferns all over the island. Birds chattered above them, reminding Angus of the seriousness of the situation in which he found himself, but for the moment, walking with Beth through the cool shadows, it was hard to think of doom or disaster. He found instead a contentment he hadn't felt for three long years.

'See,' she said, as they came into a clearing and he saw a wooden hut, the timber silvered by time and sunlight, wide French windows open at the front so the deck and living room were one. A faded red and white canvas chair was pulled close to the edge of the deck, beside a table that appeared to have been made out of half a barrel. And on it were scattered shells, large and small, and pieces of driftwood in silvery, sinewy shapes.

In the far side of this deck a woven hammock, green and purple, hung temptingly, while inside an ancient old couch was brightened up with a rainbow of cushions. Angus felt a hand close around his heart.

Then squeeze!

Beside the couch was a little cane chair—child size—a colleague had given them for Bobby…

He shook away the memory of the little boy—his little boy—sitting in the chair and considered colour instead.

Beth's love of colour!

He thought back to his apartment in the city, the one Beth had moved into when they'd married. A very expensive interior designer had decorated it for him only a year earlier, modern, minimalist grey, white and black. Functional!

When Beth had first moved in she'd brightened it with soft mohair throws, magazines strewn across the coffee-table, or huge bunches of vivid flowers, but as time had gone on, she'd come to confine her love of colour to Bobby's room, although an orange throw she'd left behind when she'd moved out still hung over his black leather lounge.

Apart from her touches of colour, she hadn't changed anything in his apartment, and he hadn't needed to ask why. Beth's only desire had been that he be comfortable, and he'd accepted her unobtrusive way of making sure that happened without ever questioning whether she was happy or whether making him happy had been enough for her…

'Would you like a coffee? You didn't finish your breakfast. I've cereal and fruit if you'd like some, but I take most of my meals at the medical centre or the camp, so I don't keep much in the way of food here.'

'You're doing it again,' he growled, then regretted his tone of voice as her startled gaze fixed on his face.

'Doing what?'

'Thinking of other people—me—first,' he said, grumbling now rather than growling. 'You always do it! You've been up all night, you must be exhausted, and emotionally upset as well because you *have* connected to that little boy, yet you're offering to make me coffee. Worrying that *I* didn't have breakfast. I'm willing to bet you haven't eaten either. And you've lost weight—you're way too thin. This was a stupid idea, running away like this to an island—'

'Angus?'

It wasn't so much his name as the smile that accompanied it that stopped his grouching. The smile was soft and gentle, loving even, and it hurt his chest as if it had pressed against a bruise.

'You always get cranky when you're hungry. Sit down. I'll get us both some cereal, although I suppose it's closer to lunchtime, but it's all I can offer. And tea? I'm making a pot. And I *will* rest later, but I did sleep during the night. It's just not the same, is it, the sleep you get sitting up?'

Beth hoped it didn't sound as if she was prattling on but if it wasn't bad enough having Angus in her home—her sanctuary—here he was saying things that made her think he still cared about her, cared about her health and welfare.

Weird!

Although he was a very caring person once you got past his rather stern, remote exterior.

And when his mind wasn't on other things, like work.

Although surely his mind should be on work now—on this possible pandemic…

She poured muesli into cereal bowls, sliced pawpaw from the tree just outside her door onto it, added milk then made a pot of tea. Angus, who had mooched around her tiny, cluttered living room, picking up a shell here, a glass float there, was now in the nook that served as her kitchen, so close she bumped into him as she turned to get a tray.

'Sorry,' he said, grasping her elbow to steady her.

'That's okay, it's a bit cramped,' she managed, although her skin burned where his hand had been and it took all her willpower not to throw herself into his arms and lose herself and her tiredness and her worry over Robbie and the other patients, in the strength of his arms and the warmth of his body.

Really, after three years you should be doing better than this! she scolded herself. But she doubted if a thousand years—a million—would stop her feeling the way she did about Angus.

It's physical, she tried to tell herself, but she wasn't very convincing. The physical appeal was only part of it—loving him was the hard part. Loving him and knowing her love wasn't returned. Oh, he'd been fond of her, and he'd loved Bobby, but…

She fought the memories, managing to put the bowls, spoons, cups and the teapot on the tray. He picked it up and carried it, without asking, out to the deck, moving a few shells so he could set it down on the table.

Angus looked around, saw her other deck chair folded by the wall. He picked it up, feeling slightly smug, unfolded it and set it opposite the one she used.

Surely if she had a man living here, even overnighting occasionally, she'd have two chairs on the deck, Angus decided as he settled cautiously—he knew these darned things could fold up on you in an instant—into the chair.

Then he took in the surroundings for the first time and realised he could see the pure white sand and green-blue water of the lagoon through the fringed fronds of young coconut palms.

'This is a beautiful setting,' he said, shaking his head as he realised just how beautiful it was.

Beth was smiling at him, as if she could read his surprise and was pleased by it.

'Not a bad place to run away to,' she teased, and he shook his head again.

No one had ever teased him as Beth did—gently and lovingly, but still getting under his skin.

In fact, everything about Beth got under his skin—it had happened six years ago when he'd first met her, and it was happening again. Or maybe she'd just stayed there, and he'd pushed her deep inside, trying to pretend she wasn't there at all.

He had to be careful. He didn't want that to happen again. Losing his child had been something from which a part of him would never fully recover, but losing Beth had been worse. It had disrupted his life to such an extent he'd lost his joy in work, the one thing that had always been there for him, and though he'd continued working—had worked like a madman, in fact—he'd known he hadn't been getting the results he'd got when he'd been married. Known that he'd lost the ability to find that extra connection to produce brilliant results rather than satisfactory ones.

The invitation to go to the CDC had been like a lifeline. It had given him a challenge, a new focus—something big enough to stop him thinking, remembering…

Regretting…

CHAPTER FOUR

'WHAT'S next?' Beth asked when she'd finished her late breakfast and no longer had the excuse of eating to save her making conversation.

Angus, also finished, had been looking out at the view while he drank his tea. He turned back towards her, sipped again, then sighed.

Stop thinking, Beth…

Focus.

'I've been thinking about it. I'd like to autopsy one of the dead birds.'

'You can't do that!' Beth said, fear for him making her voice too shrill, too loud. 'That's exactly how those people in the laboratory overseas died before the virus was isolated. They were studying the dead birds and didn't realise just how deadly the virus was. And that was in a lab, with at least some containment facilities. To do it here would be suicidal, Angus.'

'I do have *some* sense,' he reminded her. 'Apparently there's a lab at the park ranger station, but I doubt they'd have a lamina flow room or chimney. But gowned and gloved—'

'It's still a risk,' Beth protested, but he quietened her with a touch of his hand on her arm.

'I don't think it *is* bird flu, Beth,' he said. 'The worst avian influenza outbreaks have been in China, where millions upon millions of birds are farmed, and it is in those populations that the worst outbreaks have occurred. Chickens and ducks in particular have been susceptible and other what we might call domesticated birds like geese and even swans have been found with the virus. Where it's passed to wild birds, it's passed to those species, not crossed to other species.'

His hand had remained on her arm and now his fingers stroked her skin—absent-mindedly she knew, and she should ignore it, but the touch was soothing and electrifying at the same time.

She couldn't let Angus do this to her again! Couldn't let herself be carried away on a tide of physical sensations.

Although—

Nonsense!

She focussed on her argument.

'But it could—in fact, you can't be certain that hasn't already happened. You've said yourself no one ever knows all the latest developments in any scientific process.'

He smiled at her.

'Quoting me, Beth?'

The smile and a softness in the words made her blood swoop along her veins, but she had to maintain her poise—maintain a pretence that this was just a normal conversation with a colleague. She would *not* be swept into a bundle of dizzy desire by Angus's smiles.

Not again.

'Only because it seemed to fit.' Very mature response, that. 'And the fact remains that birds are dying.'

Angus nodded.

'I've been thinking about that and I believe there could be a simple explanation—sad, but simple.'

Beth watched him, waiting for more, so ridiculously happy to be sitting here like this with Angus she knew she should probably have herself committed to a secure ward somewhere until the madness passed.

'Are you going to tell me?' she finally asked, when the silence had stretched between them for so long she wondered—more madness—if he might be as comfortable as she was.

Another smile.

'Not yet,' he said. 'But when I know, I'll explain it all. In the meantime, you should get some sleep. I'll see you later?'

It was such a weird question, asked as if he was taking it for granted that he would—no, more than that, that he *wanted* to see her later…

How likely was that?

When she'd suggested their marriage wasn't working, he'd walked away without a second thought. So swiftly, in fact, she'd known for sure that what she'd always suspected had been true. Angus had married her because she'd been pregnant, not because he'd loved her…

But that had been then and this was now, and if it had just been a casual remark, she had to respond in kind.

'I suppose so—if you'll be around the hospital, we probably won't be able to avoid each other.'

She was looking out towards the water as she spoke and

didn't see his reaction, so when he replied, 'I was thinking more of personal contact, Beth,' she had to swing around to look at him to see if she could make out what he'd meant from some expression on his face.

Impossible! It always had been that way when she'd tried to read emotions on Angus's face.

So she had to ask.

'Why?'

His eyes scanned her face and she wondered just what he was reading there.

Fear?

Apprehension?

Hopefully not excitement!

'Would you object?'

'That's not an answer,' she managed, although her nerves were now so taut that any movement might snap them.

He sighed and rubbed his hands across his face, the way he did when he was tired, or worried about something, then turned and looked at her.

'Seeing you again,' he said, so slowly she wondered if he was testing each and every word before he said it, or if reluctance was holding them back, 'I realise how much I miss you.'

The words stopped the swooping in her blood, replacing it with song, but this was worse than madness—this reaction was stupidity. She had to stay calm, stay focussed. She'd rebuilt her life and grown to be happy in her own way. Content…

Mature!

'It's been three years, Angus, and you've just realised that?'

He lifted one shoulder in an embarrassed kind of shrug.

'I've been busy with work. You must know I can do that—can get so involved with it, nothing else matters.'

'Yes, I know,' Beth said quietly, then she stood up, stacked the dirty dishes on the tray and walked away.

Angus watched her go and wondered just which occasion when he'd been too 'involved' had sprung into her mind. When she'd phoned to say her labour pains were down to three minutes apart and he'd suggested she get a cab to the hospital and he'd meet her there?

Even this long after the event, remorse and shame stabbed through him.

He *had* met her there eventually, though for an hour he'd used an important phase of an experiment at work as an excuse to not go, afraid that seeing Beth in pain might be too much for him to bear. Afraid of how he might react to her pain—afraid of emotion—that dangerous X factor he'd been trained by his father, and his own childhood experience, to not feel.

And by the time he had arrived, she'd been in trouble, the cord twisted around Bobby's neck, everyone too frantic for any talk, everyone intent on saving the infant.

Saving Bobby…

Beth rinsed the dishes and set them on the sink to wash later, then considered washing them now in order to prolong the time before she had to face Angus again. The problem wasn't her pathetic reaction to Angus's words—his admission that he'd missed her—although singing in the blood was bad enough, but why Angus would say such a thing?

Angus never said anything that might be even vaguely

indicative of his feelings. In fact, at times, early in their marriage, she'd wondered if he had feelings—if perhaps his extraordinary intelligence had somehow taken up the space where feelings should have been.

But then she'd seen him with Bobby—seen the gentleness in his hands as he'd held his little son, seen the way he'd smiled at the little boy, and stroked his head and cheek when he'd been fretful.

So, yes, he did have feelings.

But for her? Or did 'missing her' simply mean he missed the convenience of a wife—someone to cut his grapefruit in the mornings?

She was thinking she *had* to return to the deck, when the phone rang. Charles, for Angus. She carried the handpiece out to him then backed away, not wanting to seem to be eavesdropping, although the conversation, on Angus's side, was unrevealing. Two 'Right's and an 'Okay' before he stood up and brought the phone into the living room where she was sitting on the couch.

'I'm going back to the medical centre,' he said, hovering beside her, eventually taking a deep breath before adding, 'I'll call in here after I finish.'

Finish?

Beth was about to ask, when she remembered his talk of autopsying one of the dead birds. She leapt to her feet.

'You're not still thinking of looking at one of the dead birds, are you?'

Had she sounded too anxious—manic?—that he smiled?

'I'll take every precaution,' he assured her, 'but you must admit it might be the fastest and easiest way to allay everyone's fears.'

'But how? You'd still have to send samples from the bird to the mainland for testing. You can't tell just from looking at the inside of a bird what it died from—unless it was strangled and had petechiae or some other indicator of cause of death.'

'Exactly,' Angus said. 'Something like starvation—that should be obvious. Birds don't suffer from anorexia.'

'Starvation?' Beth echoed, but Angus was already crossing the deck, though he paused at the top of the steps, turning around and lifting his hand in a half-wave.

'I'll see you later,' he said, then leapt the two steps onto the soft sand, striding briskly away before Beth could again ask why.

It was useless to speculate on exactly what was prompting Angus's behaviour, so Beth focussed on the earlier conversation.

'Starvation?' she muttered to herself. Here on an island with abundant life all around it? Most of the birds lived on shellfish, of which there were plenty, so how could they possibly be dying of starvation?

She reached up to the bookshelf behind her and found her bird book, seeking the chapter on shearwaters.

Migratory, she knew that. It was because they were migratory, flying north for the Arctic summer then returning south to breed, that bird flu had loomed as a possibility in her mind. The birds' path took them across Siberia, Korea, China and Southeast Asia. Stopping to feed in any of these places, they could have picked up the virus.

Although according to Angus, ducks gave it to ducks and chickens to chickens, so *was* it possible for shearwaters to pick it up on their way south?

Realising she had no idea, or any way of finding out, she headed for her bedroom. Sleep would do little to clear away her confusion over Angus's behaviour, and certainly wouldn't provide answers to her bird queries, but it would make her better able to deal with whatever lay ahead of her on this confusing day.

Angus made his way back to the medical centre with long, swift strides—trying to escape the strange emotions that had come upon him in Beth's little hut. Had he really told her he missed her—revealed his confused emotional state to her?

He had, but was that all bad?

Wasn't it not talking about their emotions that had brought them to the end of their marriage?

Hadn't they already discussed this earlier?

So telling her must be good.

Mustn't it?

As he neared the new building, he realised he might be creating an impression of urgency which could panic someone watching him, and deliberately slowed his pace.

But taking shorter steps didn't make it easier to switch his thoughts from Beth to science, although now he'd mentioned starvation—thinking aloud as he'd talked to her—something was niggling in his brain, something to do with flight paths of migratory birds.

Focus.

Think.

Where?

Korea, he rather thought, teasing at the idea, sure if it was an article he'd read, he'd be able to recall it word for word as his memory was visual.

Had it been something he'd heard?

'So much for keeping it quiet,' Charles said gloomily as Angus, still trying to recall the snippet of information, walked into the medical centre office. 'The phone's ringing off the hook—journalists wanting a story. Next thing we know there'll be news helicopters hovering overhead, all looking to photograph dead birds. We're trying to contact all the parents of children who are at the camp without their families, so we can allay their fears before they hear or see a news report, but that's not easy, with so many parents at work.'

'Have you someone competent who can handle the press calls?' Angus asked, and Charles smiled.

'Fortunately, we have an excess of staff available. It might not have come from her training as a cardiac surgeon, but Gina Jamieson is a genius at using a lot of words to say nothing. *And* she's got an American accent so she sounds as if she really knows things. All the press calls are going to her.'

'And the vaccination programme?'

'Will get under way as soon as stocks of vaccine arrive. In the meantime, the Australian Quarantine and Inspection Service has contacted the army, who will fly in a mobile bio-hazard laboratory and a mobile decontamination unit to Crocodile Creek. An army helicopter will then airlift them to the island. Both units should be here tomorrow afternoon at the latest.'

'Are they sending personnel—scientists?'

Charles shook his head, then he smiled at Angus.

'They seem to think they've got one of the best on site.

You spent some time at the Centers for Disease Control and Prevention in Atlanta recently?'

Angus nodded. Like epidemiologists the world over, he'd jumped at the chance to spend time in the world's premier disease-control centre, and one of the things he'd studied there had been the genetics of the bird flu virus. But then his learning had been theoretical.

Putting what he knew into practice was different…

Testing without an MChip was different…

The bed was too hot, or maybe it was too soft. Beth tossed and turned, telling herself she had to sleep, knowing she wouldn't. In the end she forsook the bed and wandered out onto the deck, climbing cautiously into the hammock which had been known to tip her out if approached unwarily.

But there, with the salt-laden breeze cooling her skin and the smell of the reef in the air wrapping around her, she dozed.

And dreamt…

The raucous squabbles of a pair of sooty terns, fighting over a morsel of food, woke her, and she looked around blearily. Above the noise of the birds was another noise, also familiar, although why a helicopter should be circling overhead, she wasn't sure.

The small aircraft throbbed into view and tilted over the beach, then swung in a wide arc and the noise slowly faded into the distance.

Press, Beth realised. The island was already in the news. The now-familiar fear tightened her nerves, but Angus had said it probably wasn't bird flu and that the quarantine was just a precaution.

Angus!

The thought of him calmed her, and now she realised that, through the leaves of the pawpaw tree, she could see a tall figure on the beach—a bizarre sight on this tropical island, for the man was wearing a white business shirt, unbuttoned at the neck and with sleeves turned up to the elbows, and grey trousers, rolled up to just below the knees. And beside him a little boy—Sam?—running in and out of the water, splashing with his hands so the man's trousers were probably spotted with salt water.

She remembered back to what Angus had been wearing at breakfast this morning—not for him casual, tropical wear of baggy shorts and floral shirts. No, he was at a conference—working—and work wear was grey trousers and a white business shirt.

But Angus paddling? Splashing with a little boy? Angus?

She remembered thinking that morning that he'd changed, but paddling? For that was what the man was undoubtedly doing. Sloshing through the shallow water at the edge of the lagoon, bending over to splash water at the child and looking, for all the world, as if he was enjoying it.

She tipped herself out of the hammock and went to join them, passing Angus's shoes set neatly by her bottom step, *her* bare feet enjoying the crunchy texture of the coarse coral sand on the path down to the beach.

'You were sleeping,' he said, as she drew closer, and Sam greeted her with a shout.

'You could have come in anyway,' she told him, uncertain now she was closer just why she'd come.

'Your little friend was heading for the beach. He tells

me he's supposed to be in the hall, having quiet time. I did check with one of the carers—Mrs Someone, an older woman—who said as long as he stayed with me and kept his hat on, he could play in the water. Actually…' He smiled as he added, 'The water tempted me as well.'

Ordinary enough words but something in his voice suggested a subtext in the phrase.

She studied him, then smiled back at him, certain he couldn't have meant anything more than he'd said—certainly not that seeing her asleep had tempted him in some way.

'And Charles? You're not wanted at the medical centre? You've given up the idea of autopsying a dead bird?'

'Until tomorrow,' he told her, and although he explained about the containment laboratory and the precautions they would put in place, her heart still filled with fear for him.

'So, are you free until then? Would you like a lift back to the hotel? Sam would come for a drive, wouldn't you, Sam? Or would you like to have a look around, see the camp and meet some more of the staff and kids? You could stay to dinner.'

Was she mad, suggesting this? Finding ways to keep him there, when every minute, every second with him reminded her of what she'd lost?

'I'd like to see the camp. Do I need my shoes?'

She looked down at his feet, narrow and white—feet quite unused to walking barefoot around an island, walking barefoot anywhere.

Aristocratic feet, she'd always thought.

As if aristocratic feet would look any different from ordinary feet! Feet were feet.

'Share the joke?' he asked, and Beth realised she must have been smiling at her foolishness.

'I was thinking about feet,' she offered, but didn't add whose feet, hurrying on to say, 'You should be okay barefoot. I get around that way all the time, except at work, of course. I doubt the patients would appreciate a barefoot doctor.'

Aware she was prattling, she led him towards the camp's main buildings, the dormitories, dining room and hall where discos, concerts and general fun took place, Sam darting ahead, then dashing back behind them, always on the move.

'Where is everyone, Sam?' she asked, taking his hand to stop the dizzying movement so now the three of them walked along the path.

'Hall! Listening to music, silly music—some old fellow who's dead. And watching some slides of the birds.'

'After lunch is quiet time,' Beth explained to Angus. 'They can go to their rooms or dormitories for a rest, or to the hall where they loll around, look at movies, listen to music or someone reads a story.'

She sighed.

'Poor kids—this is supposed to be a really fun time for them, going out on the reef, walking through the rain-forest at night, spotting the night animals—they came here for an adventure, not to get sick.'

'Those who are well can still enjoy the programmes surely,' Angus said, removing from Sam's hands a stick he had picked up before he could behead a bright flower from a shrub beside the path.

'Yes, they can,' Beth agreed, but she still felt the fun had been blighted—the joy of camp diminished somehow.

'Obviously there are competent support staff,' Angus said, poking his head into one of the older huts now used for arts and crafts. 'How many do they have? And who provides them?'

'The organisation sending the kids sends one person—we've got Miranda, who is a respiratory physician, with the chest group, and Benita with the cancer kids. Then Crocodile Creek Hospital supplies more support staff—Susie, our physio, and usually an occupational therapist as well. On top of that are local volunteers, people from Crocodile Creek who've been involved since the beginning—a guy who's a crocodile hunter—'

'Bruce, he's my friend and he's going to take me crocodile hunting before we go home,' Sam said, jumping up and down in anticipated excitement.

'A crocodile hunter? Surely crocodiles are protected,' Angus protested, and Beth flashed him a smile, shaking her head to warn him not to spoil Sam's fun.

'They are, but if you're a tourist from overseas and you want to see crocodiles in their natural habitat, do you want to go out in a boat with a guide or with someone who calls himself a crocodile hunter?'

She spoke quietly, but Sam had dashed ahead again, maybe in search of Bruce, entering a hall not much farther along the track.

Angus returned Beth's smile, reminding her of the folly of being close to him any more than was absolutely necessary. But it also made her feel warm and happy inside—almost complete…

And she'd missed him *so* much…

'So Bruce—that's hardly the name for a crocodile-hunter hero, is it?—is a volunteer, and I suppose the others are equally unlikely.'

'They are. There's the mayor and sometimes the CEO of the sugar mill—his son Harry is in charge of the local police station. Harry's married to Grace, the nurse you met at the hospital this morning.'

'And I've met Harry as well. He flew in this morning to ensure the quarantine order is carried out—he's the official heavyweight, from what I can gather.'

They'd reached the hall, carefully constructed to withstand future cyclones but looking as if it had grown among the palm trees, a building at one with its surroundings.

'The dormitories, girls' and boys', are over there.' Beth waved her hand to the two equally well-designed buildings. 'And the dining room is behind them. The paths here, as you can see, are compacted sand to make wheelchair access easier. I'm sorry, I'd forgotten that—is the surface rough on your feet?'

Angus heard the anxious note in her voice and wanted to shake her—gently—to tell her she had to stop worrying about other people quite so much. But that was Beth and nothing would change her, and his urge to shake turned into an urge to hug.

But hugs would lead to other urges that were already causing some concern, not in his body which was revelling in this contact with his ex-wife, but in his head, where images of Beth he thought he'd excised years ago were now flashing on a memory screen.

Beth serving him a hot, delicious meal at midnight

when he'd come in from work so tired and frazzled the last thing he'd wanted to do was eat. Yet he'd known he had to so he'd sat, and while he'd eaten, she'd massaged his shoulders and neck, her fingers easing out the knots of strain until, well fed and more relaxed, he'd been able to take her on his knee and feel the rest of the frustration of the day disappear from his body, lost in the softness that was Beth.

He watched her as she walked through the open door into the big hall, its walls decorated with huge posters showing coral and bright fish, reminders everywhere that they were in a national park and not to touch animals or plants in the water or on the land.

Inside, children and teenagers sat or lay in groups on the floor, some talking, some listening to stories. No dead person's music that Angus could hear, although Sam had attached himself to a man in a battered hat—so battered Angus suspected it had holes poked in it by a sharp knife to represent a tussle with crocodile teeth.

One of the older camp kids, a teenage boy with the blond-streaked hair of a surfer, saw them come in. Angus saw him prod the girl beside him, a pretty teenager, the baseball cap backwards on her head suggesting recent chemo.

'Here's Beth,' the lad called out. 'Dance for us, Beth.'

The girl clapped her hands, starting a movement that ran around the room.

'Dance, Beth, dance, Beth!' The kids clapped and chanted and though Beth smiled it was forced, while the look she sent to Angus was one of pure, anguished apology.

'I'm sorry. We shouldn't have come here—this is silly—but I can't say no, you can see that. The kids…'

Her shoulders lifted in a rueful shrug, and with a final tormented smile at Angus she made her way to the front of the hall, where Sam, deserting his mate, now joined her, a toy dog in his hands.

Without looking at it, Angus could have described the toy—a brown dog, dressed in a top hat and tails, its front paws holding drumsticks, a drum in front of it. And as Sam pressed the button to start the music, Angus felt his heart contract into a hard, tight lump. The first time he'd seen Beth she'd been in the children's ward at the hospital, dancing to the beat of a similar drumming dog, singing along with it. A year later he'd surprised her by buying another copy of the toy for Bobby and it had become his favourite, so he'd gone to sleep each night to the dog beating out the toe-tapping tune, 'Putting on the Ritz'.

Had Beth bought this particular toy for the kids' camp? Angus suspected she had, for it certainly wasn't Bobby's dog. Bobby's dog was—

'Start the music again, Sam,' Beth was saying. 'I'll only dance if all of you who know the steps get up with me,' she said, and a knot of small children scampered out to join her.

'Go on, Star,' the surfie-looking lad said to the girl beside him.

'Not yet,' she said. 'I will eventually because Beth's so patient, just not yet.'

And to Angus's surprise, the young lad reached over and took the girl's hand, whispering, though loudly enough for Angus to hear. 'I know you will!'

But familiar music at the front of the room diverted Angus's attention from the young couple.

And as Beth tap-danced across the front of the room, her hands clapping to produce the taps her bare feet couldn't, he understood her fractured sentences earlier and the worry that had stained her voice, but, watching, he thought not of Bobby but of the day he'd met Bobby's mother…

The day she'd tap-danced her way into his heart.

Except that he hadn't realised that's where she had been until it was too late and both she and Bobby were gone.

And he had been left with his work…

CHAPTER FIVE

HE WALKED out of the hall, making his way back to the beach, not wanting to see Beth—not wanting her to see him and divine the emotion the silly drum-beating dog had aroused in him.

A dead bird lay in the centre of the path, and he felt the scrunch of panic in his chest. It was well within the boundaries of the camp. What if one of the children had picked it up?

He felt in his pocket, sure there'd be a plastic bag, but, no, he was on a holiday island—at a conference—so why would he be carrying plastic bags? The dining room must be close—Beth had said it was behind the dormitories—but in the meantime there was the bird.

'Ah, another one.'

He turned to see an elderly man behind him. The man was dragging a large garbage bag and carrying a tool road-cleaners used to pick up rubbish from the verges. He pressed the handle so the jaws at the end of the long tool opened, then clamped them around the bird and dumped it into his bag.

Angus watched with a mix of horror and relief.

'The rangers are supposed to be collecting the dead birds,' he protested. 'And they're supposed to be wearing protective covering and masks. You should be, too, if you're picking up dead birds.'

'It's not bird flu,' the man said, and he sounded so sure of himself Angus was inclined to believe him, though for no scientific reason at all. 'They're falling out of the sky, the birds. I've been watching. It's not the birds that got here safely that are sick, but the ones still coming in. The fishermen out on the reef have seen it, too. Now, I'm no fancy scientist but it seems to me birds sick with bird flu would have died before they got this far. Say they got sick in China on the way, they wouldn't have had the strength to fly for another week to get here, now, would they? I reckon these birds aren't sick, they're exhausted.'

Again the memory of hearing something about birds and exhaustion tickled in Angus's head but he still couldn't grasp the significance of it. In the meantime, this man seemed to know what he was talking about.

'Do you live here on the island?' he asked, and the man shook his head, then extended his hand.

'Grubb's m'name but people call me Grubby—don't mind that they do. The wife and I, we work at the hospital over on the mainland—have done for more'n forty years. Met there when we were youngsters, got married forty years ago. Charles, he reckons we should celebrate the anniversary, gives us time off, and there's nothing for it, Mrs Grubb announces, but that we come over as volunteers for the kids. She loves the kids.'

Angus stared at the man who'd imparted a lifetime of information so succinctly, then backtracked.

'But you know something about these migratory birds?'

Grubby twisted the top on the plastic bag before answering.

'Been coming to the island for holidays since I was a kid. Was here when the university fellas tagged all the mutton birds and tracked them all the way back to Siberia in Russia—did you know that's where they go when they're not here? Funny, that, from a tropical place to snow. Course, people coming to the posh resort don't take kindly to a bird named common like a mutton bird, so they call 'em by their right name—shearwaters—now. But mutton birds they are here and always will be. Used to be a plant here that boiled them down for oil. Powerful stuff, mutton-bird oil used to be considered. Easy to catch because they burrow, you see.'

Hardly comforting news, Angus decided as Grubby departed, the sack now slung over his shoulder. How many dead birds might be hidden in the burrows? And just where was Grubby going to despatch his dead birds?

Hurrying after the man, Angus discovered he was going to the medical centre.

'I put 'em in the hazardous waste drums, seal 'em up and shove them in the freezer with the other contaminated hospital waste. Fly it out once a week because they've only got a small freezer unit here, and it's collected from the hospital on the mainland once a month.'

'Can you wait while I get my shoes? I'd like to see the process,' Angus said.

Grubby rested his sack on the ground by way of reply and waited until Angus returned, neatly shod and with his trousers rolled back down.

By the time he'd had a tour of the medical centre's disposal facilities and spoken to Charles about plans for the arrival and placement of the mobile units, it was late afternoon.

He should, by rights, return to the hotel and join his colleagues for dinner, but he found he had no desire at all for theoretical conversation when the containment of a possible epidemic was happening right here and now. He was also drawn to return to Beth's little hut, sure she'd be there now.

But that might look needy, and needy was a weakness his father had ruthlessly eliminated from Angus's nature. A man should be complete within himself, using the intelligence he had been given to programme his life to perfection. Yes, there were physical needs genetically wired into us for the survival of the species, but these could be satisfied by mutual agreement between a man and a woman. They did not have to be romanticised, or emotionalised—that way lay disaster.

Angus shuddered as his father's edicts rang so clearly in his head. How had he, Angus, an intelligent man, allowed himself to be so brainwashed?

Although he couldn't entirely blame the brainwashing. Hadn't he learned the truth himself, that day, aged seven, when he'd whispered those fatal words, 'I love you, Mum,' to his mother as he'd left for school, returning in the afternoon to find her gone…

He pushed away the memories, not wanting them hanging like a black cloud around his head, thinking he'd visit the little boy and the thick black clouds might be visible to a child.

Robbie…

The name was nothing more than coincidence, but when he entered the room and found Beth beside the little boy's bed, he knew she, too, felt the tie.

She turned at his entry, her eyes, above the blue mask she wore, dark with worry.

'No good?' Angus murmured, lifting a second chair and setting down noiselessly beside Beth's, lifting the mask that hung around his neck and fastening it into place.

'No good at all. He's lapsing in and out of consciousness, and then Danny, one of the other children who'd been isolated, has been admitted following a seizure. Then there's Lily—Alex, the guest who's a neurosurgeon, did a lumbar puncture on her yesterday afternoon.'

Robbie was tossing and turning on the bed, at times muttering feverishly then quietening, before the muttering began again.

'The earlier test results not back?' Angus asked, and Beth shook her head.

'Apparently there was some mix-up and they were sent to Brisbane rather than being done locally, then the containers were lost at the lab.' The words were muffled by the mask but the story familiar enough. Why was it always the important specimens or slides that went missing? 'Charles has spent hours on the phone this afternoon, trying to chase them down. I think he's found where they are and is pushing for a result asap. On top of that, he's desperately concerned about Lily.'

'Depending on the facilities in this mobile lab they're sending, I could do the tests here tomorrow.'

He sounded quite cheerful about it, but Beth couldn't

help feeling guilty. She was feeling a lot of other things as well, with Angus so close, but guilt was the only one she could consider right now.

'I'm sorry I got you into this,' she said. 'But you don't have to stay involved. I know Charles must have been enormously grateful to have someone like you to back him up over the steps he had to take, but now things are all under way, you could go back to your conference.'

Angus was watching Robbie, stroking the little boy's arm with the tip of his gloved forefinger. Beth waited for him to turn, to look at her, but when he answered, he kept his eyes on the sick child in the bed.

'I'll be needed here tomorrow when the lab arrives,' he said. 'So I may as well stay. Problem is, Charles tells me accommodation on this side of the island is fully booked. Am I right in thinking that old couch of yours folds out into a bed?'

Beth heard the words—and none of them were complex or difficult to understand—but taken together they didn't make a lot of sense.

Well, they did, but the sense they made filled her with apprehension.

'You want to stay here? On this side? It's only fifteen minutes in a cart from the resort where you've got a comfortable bed, yet you'd sleep on my old couch?'

'I'd rather be close to the action,' he said, still not looking at her, but Beth could feel it now, the physical attraction that had stirred between them from their first meeting. It was filtering beneath her skin, and teasing alert the hairs on her arms. It was heating tissues deep inside her, and making her breasts ache with wanting.

'Just close to the action?' she whispered, accenting the final word only slightly.

Now he looked at her, his hazel eyes meeting hers, a slight flush on his cheeks.

Sun-kissed from his walk on the beach or something else?

'No,' he said, but she'd forgotten what she'd asked, so caught up in the physical heat that had drawn her to Angus from the beginning, her mind was barely functioning.

'Mu-u-u-m!'

Robbie's tortured cry broke the spell, and Beth bent over the child, whispering to him, holding his shoulders until the convulsive thrashing stopped.

'That's the first coherent word he's spoken,' she said to Angus, her voice breaking with the pain she felt for the sick child. 'And his mum can't be here with him.'

'He's barely conscious and probably doesn't realise that,' Angus said, putting his arm around Beth's shoulder and giving her a comforting hug, while she used a damp cloth to wipe the sweat from Robbie's face. 'Why don't you take a break? I'll sit with him for a while.'

'No, you can both go.'

The voice made them both turn, and Beth smiled when she saw Marcia in the doorway.

'Angus, this is Marcia, one of the nurses from the mainland hospital. Marcia, Angus. But, Marcia, aren't you running the kids' camp trivia contest tonight?'

'It's been cancelled and they're having a movie instead—James Bond, especially for the older boys. Not to mention an excuse to have popcorn. So I'm here to tell you that Robbie's mine for the next few hours. Remember

I'm the one he came to when he felt sick—I'm the one who looks like his mum. So off you go. You can come back later, Beth, but you know he'll be in good hands if you actually decide to have a decent night's sleep.'

She glanced from Beth to Angus, seeming to focus on Angus's arm still around Beth's shoulders.

'Or not,' she added blithely, before hiding her smile behind her mask and coming farther into the room.

Would Beth tell him to return to the hotel?

Angus found he didn't have a clue how she would react, but then, growing up as she had, in and out of foster-homes all her life, she'd learned, too well, to hide her feelings.

Though she had shown them in her anxiety to please, in her quiet determination to do whatever she could to make others around her happy.

'The dining room will be closed but I can get some fish or steaks from the kitchen and rustle up a salad. Would that do you for dinner?'

The question told him she'd accepted his decision to stay and it was all he could do not to do a little tap-dance himself, except that, try as she had, Beth had never been able to teach him the steps.

'Do you have a barbeque? And do we get a choice when you're pinching things from the kitchen? I'm probably a better steak cook than a fish cook.'

She turned to smile at him.

'You're probably equally proficient with both,' she said, smiling at him. 'Apart from tap-dancing, I doubt there's anything you've ever set your mind to do and not succeeded.'

He shook his head, surprised to find their thoughts had been so in tune. Though it had often been that way—to such an extent he'd sometimes wondered if it was their mutual difficulty in expressing their emotions that had led to them communicating through their thoughts.

Though back then he'd dismissed such ideas as fanciful.

'Perhaps steak. I had fish last night.'

They'd reached the building behind the dormitories and although most of it was in darkness, a light shone above a door at the back. Beth produced a bunch of keys, selected a bright pink one and unlocked the door.

'It's like the corner store,' she said. 'All the staff have access. We write down what we take, and get a monthly bill. Far easier than trying to work out what food we want sent across from the mainland.'

She moved easily around the big kitchen, picking up a plastic carry basket and stacking her selection into it—plastic-wrapped meat from a cool-room, mushrooms, an avocado, some green leaves in a plastic bag, tiny tomatoes and, with a smile directed at Angus, a couple of onions.

'Can't have steak without onions,' she teased, quoting him again, the smile in her voice making him feel comfortable and confused at the same time.

Surely they couldn't be slotting so easily back into each other's lives—not after parting as they had, both of them lost in bitter grief they hadn't been able to verbalise or share.

And surely there was danger here, danger in the feeling of comfort into which he was sinking—as dangerous as quicksand, the sinking as inevitable. Yet the pleasure of simply being with Beth—being in her undemanding company—was too much to resist, so thoughts of danger were pushed away and the warning signals ringing in his head were ruthlessly ignored.

Back at her little hut, she produced not a regular gas-fired barbeque but a small, cast-iron brazier, with space for heat beads in the bottom and a grilling rack and hot plate combination on the top.

'The single woman's barbeque,' she said, putting it down on a side table and lighting the beads. 'Though it's big enough for two steaks. Do you want to slice the onions while it heats?'

The question surprised him, reminding him it had been three years since he and Beth had lived together. That Beth would have sliced the onions herself, protesting, if he'd offered, that she'd liked to fuss over him.

And as he followed her into the kitchen he wasn't sure just what he felt about this change—small enough but indicative that this Beth was a stranger, no matter how familiar she seemed.

Big mistake, suggesting he slice the onions, Beth realised as he followed her into the tiny space that was her kitchen.

She tried to stay as small as possible as she washed the salad leaves and whirled them dry, then cut the avocado into slices, but inevitably they brushed against each other and when, the onions neatly sliced, Angus swung around to wash his hands, they collided. His wrists—oniony hands held carefully away—caught her shoulders to steady her and their eyes met, then their lips, the kiss a question and a confirmation.

Was this what they wanted?

The magic was still there…

'Onion hands,' Angus said, breaking away.

'And I've squashed the avocado,' Beth managed, though she was sure she didn't sound as composed as Angus had. 'I'll have to make it into dressing now.'

She studied the solid back of her ex-husband as he, very efficiently, washed his hands at the sink. The kiss had suggested that he'd been feeling the same residual attraction she'd been feeling since they'd met that morning, but was that all it was—remembered physical delight?

Assuming it was, the best thing to do was to ignore it.

And maybe scrape the avocado off her fingers before she spread it all around the cabin…

'I'll put the onions on first,' Angus said, turning from the sink, her small pumpkin-shaped and -coloured hand-towel in his hands. 'A plate for when they're cooked?'

She pulled out a drawer where her assortment of crockery, mostly found at flea markets and antique shops, was kept and handed him one, wishing that particular one hadn't been on top—who knew what Angus would think of a Donald Duck souvenir plate from Disneyland via the farmers' market at Eumundi?

Not her, certainly, because, although he'd raised an eyebrow at her as he'd looked at it, he made no comment, simply carrying it, the bowl of sliced onions and the steak out to the deck.

How could she ever have believed their marriage would work? That plate was symbolic of the differences between them—Angus's crockery had all been perfectly matched, square white plates and square black plates, varying in size so they could sit on each other in black and white harmony or stand alone—a black dinner service or a white one. Not a Donald Duck plate in sight!

But when she carried the tray with the salad bowl, cutlery and two more plates out to the table, the sight of Angus bent over her small barbeque seemed so right that for a moment she forgot to breathe.

Beyond him the sky had darkened with the sudden tropical nightfall, and the paler blur of the sea was the only demarcation between the earth and the heavens. And Angus stood there, solid, concentrated, complete within himself. It had been the completeness that had fascinated Beth—and she, who'd been such a mess of insecurities, had been drawn to him as the ocean tides were drawn to the moon.

Inevitably.

Irresistibly.

'Still medium-rare?'

The man she'd been watching turned as he asked the question. She nodded her response, too afraid to speak, the secret heart of her wondering if this time it could be different—

There was no *this time*, she told herself crossly. This was ships-passing-in-the-night stuff, a chance encounter, nothing more. The crisis would be over and, like the mobile decontamination unit, Angus would depart—leaving no way to decontaminate herself if she was foolish enough to fall in love with him again.

Again?

Admit it—*still* was the word.

She still loved Angus…

No! It was attraction, nothing more. She was still *attracted* to Angus!

Liar!

The smell of the barbeque, meat and onions filled the night air, reminding Beth her meals today had been scanty to say the least. She shifted shells to make room at the table and set two places, a strange feeling of displacement settling over her as she considered she and Angus sitting down to dinner in this unlikely setting.

Though the setting was no more unlikely than her and Angus sitting down to dinner together somewhere else, given how far apart they'd been when they'd parted.

'Smells wonderful.'

The voice came out of the darkness but Beth recognised it.

'Doing some spotlighting, Jamie?' she asked, as the young lad came into the light of the deck, Stella Vavunis by his side.

'No, just giving Star some extra practice with her leg. It's easier for her to do it when the others aren't around. Although most of the others are encouraging, there are a couple of kids staying over at the resort who come to the lagoon to swim and they freak her out. And it's especially hard for her to walk on the sand, so we're going down to the beach.'

Beth smiled at the young couple.

'Nothing to do with the fact that the full moon will be rising shortly,' she teased, and Stella laughed.

'I think all Jamie knows about the full moon is that it brings good surf conditions,' she said, teasing Jamie in her turn.

'Well, have fun, the two of you,' Beth said as they moved away, Jamie with his arm around Stella's waist, presumably to steady her as she walked on her new prosthetic leg.

'Cancer?' Angus asked as he came to the table and divided the steak and onions between two plates.

'It was in the bone. She lost her lower leg. She's an example of how good the camp can be for kids—when she arrived she was determined not to use the prosthesis, insisting on wearing jeans and using crutches, but Susie, the Crocodile Creek physio, has been working not only on her muscle co-ordination but on her self-esteem, and she's done wonders.'

'I imagine young Jamie hasn't hurt her self-esteem either,' Angus said, nodding to where the pair were now heading for the harder sand at the edge of the water. 'He's some young man, to be prepared to help her the way he is.'

Beth nodded.

'I suppose, having been through cancer treatment himself, he has more understanding than a lot of kids his age. Or maybe he was always going to be a very special young man. Whatever, he's been great and Stella—he calls her Star—has blossomed under his friendship.'

'Young love!' Angus said softly, then he looked across the table at Beth.

'Did you ever feel it?'

She had just sliced off a piece of meat and balanced it and some onion rings on her fork, when Angus asked the question.

Only when I met you, didn't seem like an appropriate answer, for she'd been past young at twenty-five, but that had been exactly how she'd felt—like a giddy, dizzy teenager plunged into something she didn't fully understand.

She shook her head.

'I was moving around too much. I started my teens with a foster-family in Brisbane, then my grandmother in Gympie decided she wanted me, then I went back to a different foster-family. Moving around meant I missed school so I was always trying to catch up on schoolwork.'

'Yet you still qualified for medical school.'

Angus spoke so quietly Beth had to look at him to make sure she'd heard it right.

'Of course. I'm sure I told you some time that being a doctor was my only ambition. I was five when I had to have my tonsils and adenoids out and the doctor I was taken to was so kind and gentle I knew right from then that one day I'd be a doctor and be kind and gentle to little kids.'

Angus *had* heard the story, but hearing it again made something shift in his chest at the idea of a child so young deciding on an ambition because a stranger had been kind to her.

How little kindness must she have known that this had made such an impression?

She might talk about the benevolence of her foster-families and protest that she had never been ill-treated, but neither had she been loved.

And if anyone deserved to be loved, it was Beth.

Which, now he remembered, had been why he'd walked away from their marriage without argument. Because Beth, of all people, deserved more than a man who didn't know how to love…

Not properly…

Not the way Beth deserved to be loved…

He was eating and thinking about this, when the wail of a baby nearby stopped his fork on the way to his mouth.

'A baby? Do you have babies in the camp?'

Beth smiled across the table at him.

'That's the cry of the shearwaters. Now it's dark they'll start up—you'll hear them all night.'

'They cry like babies and burrow into the ground to nest—what else do they do, these strange birds?'

'Well, to me the marvel of them is that the adults migrate before the young are strong enough to fly all the way to Siberia, yet the young know where to go, and no doubt where to stop on the way to feed.'

'Ah! Light-bulb moment. Thank you, Beth. It's been bothering me all day, something I'd read or heard about our migratory birds, and you mentioning feeding places brought it back. Apparently there are tidal flats on the Korean peninsula where a lot of migratory birds break their journey to Australia, and recently the flats were closed off by a wall, millions of shellfish died and migrating birds were left without food for their migration. Maybe Grubby is right—the birds *are* dying of starvation.'

'Grubby? You've met Grubby?'

Beth sounded a little lost so Angus had to smile and touch her reassuringly on the hand.

And having touched her, surely leaving his hand covering hers for a short time wouldn't hurt.

'I have indeed, and now, if you've finished eating, why don't we, too, walk down to the beach—maybe not in the direction Stella and Jamie took—and watch the moon rise over the water?'

Beth stared at him, unable to believe Angus had suggested something so romantic.

Or why!

Though maybe it wasn't romance he was thinking of—maybe the moon might help him remember more about the feeding habits of migratory birds on tidal flats in Korea.

And although her head told her that walking on the beach in the moonlight with Angus was little short of madness, her heart assured her head it could handle it this time. After all, Angus was no longer her first love. She had changed, matured, become so much more sure of herself, as a doctor and as a woman. She could handle a little romance on the beach.

If that's what he had in mind…

She stacked the dirty dishes on the tray and carried them inside, noticing the breakfast things still waiting to be washed.

Do them now, common sense suggested, but Angus had followed her inside with the salad bowl and when she turned he took her in his arms and her last rational thought was that they probably wouldn't see the moon rise this particular night.

Kissing Angus was so familiar yet so different. She recognised the taste of him, the texture of his lips, recognised, too, her body's reaction—the heat, sizzling deep inside her, shafting downwards. Yet the way he held her, gently, barely touching her, as if expecting her to pull away at any moment—that was different.

But how could she pull away when the spell Angus had cast over her from the first time they'd kissed still held her firmly in its grip?

'Angus.'

She breathed his name against his lips and felt hers whispered back. Just so had they always made love—

silently—nothing but their names confirming their identities as if in kissing, touching, loving they might lose themselves and need to know again just who they were.

His arms engulfed her, wrapping her in the security of his body, holding her close so all her doubts and fears and uncertainties were kept at bay. This, too, had always been the way. Safe in Angus's arms she'd lost the insecurities that had plagued her all her life, living for the moment, living, eventually, for him, and then for Bobby…

His lips were tracing kisses down her neck, then up again, resting where her pulse beat—wildly and erratically she was sure. They found her mouth again and claimed it, a kiss so deep it drew all air from her lungs and left her gasping, clinging, wanting more than kisses.

Could he still read her so well that he lifted her into his arms, carrying her as easily as if she were a child into the bedroom where she'd tossed and turned hours earlier?

He lowered her onto the bed and knelt beside her, brushing back her hair, repeating her name, a note of wonder she hadn't heard before in his voice.

But that short journey had brought doubts in its trail—what was she doing? How could she think of rushing back into—into what? It was hardly a relationship.

Soft kisses—exploratory—moved across her skin, her name a mantra on Angus's lips.

She could barely think, and what was Angus doing? Thinking Angus, who was so controlled.

Angus, who always thought things through…

Or nearly always.

Angus—the man she'd loved—

Still loved?

She supposed so, but that didn't mean…

Thoughts twisted in her head as she kissed and was kissed, thoughts doing nothing to stop the hunger rising in her like a king tide, threatening to lift her on its curling waves and carry her to a far-off shore.

His hands roved across her breasts, encountering nipples already peaking with desire, his fingers, thumbs teasing at the tight nubs, shooting messages of desire through her body.

Then her name became a question.

'Beth?'

His hands at the buttons on her blouse…

Instead of answering, she sat up and stripped it off, over her head, then began to unbutton his staid white shirt, pushing back the edges so she could touch his skin.

Thoughts befuddled now by wanting Angus, tiny messages trying to get through—whispering in the back of her mind.

Her fingers trembled, so great was her need. They fumbled with his buttons so Angus stood and stripped off his clothes, too, joining her on the bed as she wriggled out of shorts and knickers, needing to feel his skin on hers, to be close to him all over. Wrapped in Angus once again…

But he took his time, teasing her, letting her tease him, hands grazing skin as they explored and remembered, little touches, kisses, sensations Beth had totally forgotten, desire enhanced by waiting until it became greedily demanding, their kisses hot and hard, their hands frantic in their touching.

'I want to be inside you,' Angus whispered, voice hoarse

with the hunger they'd generated—had always generated between them.

For an answer Beth shifted, lifting her hips to ease his entry, clutching at his arms in an attempt to keep herself centred, then as his erection touched her—probed—some echo of the past returned, faint at first then yelling at her.

Yelling a warning about falling back into bed like this, as if there'd been no parting, no divorce, no Bobby—

Bobby!

'No, Angus, wait, it's not safe.'

She slid away from under him, so embarrassed she wanted to shrivel up and disappear, but Angus had reacted differently, sitting up and snapping on her bedside light, a look of fury on his face.

'Are you still obsessed about not having another child? Is that what this is all about? Do you lead other men on then pull away or do they come prepared with condoms? And why, in heaven's name, if you're so damned determined to remain childless, wouldn't you be on the Pill? You're a doctor—it isn't that difficult for you to get them.'

Beth stared at him, totally bewildered by his anger.

'Angus, we're not married,' she said, lamely pointing out the obvious. 'And I wasn't thinking of not having another child, but of repeating the same mistake I made last time—of getting pregnant and putting you in a position where you felt you had to marry me.'

Her voice sounded very small, even to her own ears, and perhaps Angus hadn't heard it, for he continued to pull on his clothes with a haste that suggested he couldn't wait to get out of her hut.

Holding his shoes in one hand, he headed for the door, muttering now, but words Beth couldn't hear. Then, just as she was resigned to him walking out and probably never talking to her again, he turned, glared at her, and said, 'I didn't *have* to marry you!'

CHAPTER SIX

ACCEPTING, after an hour of fruitless tossing and turning, that she wasn't going to sleep, Beth got up and headed for the shower. She'd go back up and relieve Marcia by Robbie's bed.

As water splashed down on her head, anxiety for the children who were supposed to be having a wonderful holiday simmered inside her, although it had been subdued for a while by the turbulent emotions Angus's return into her life had caused.

But now he was gone again—his departure unmistakably final, so even if she did see him around the place, they would be meeting as colleagues, not almost-lovers.

She soaped her body all over, rubbing at her skin, actions automatic as her mind followed the trail of Angus.

No, she was damned if she was going to sigh over what had happened. Bad enough that she'd lost sleep.

So what if she and Angus were still attracted to each other?

So what if she'd upset him by her sudden refusal to make love?

Shampoo bubbles cascaded down her face.

She'd upset herself as well—badly—wanting him, aching for him, yet not lost enough in lust to risk what had happened before.

And if he thought she'd pulled away because of what he called her obsession to not have another child, then he could go on thinking that. Better that he thought her a little batty than realised just how much guilt she'd carried over that first pregnancy.

Lifting her head, she let the water stream down her face, hiding tears she wasn't going to admit were there, rinsing out the conditioner from her hair.

By the time she'd dried herself off, combed the tangles from her hair and dressed in clean clothes, she was Dr Beth Stuart again, competent medical practitioner, in charge of the new Wallaby Island Medical Centre.

Mature!

This façade crumpled only slightly when she reached Robbie's bed and found Angus sitting beside the pale, still child.

Beth stood inside the door, wanting to turn away but knowing it was too late.

'I've nothing better to do so I thought I might sit with him for a while. Being in the centre helps me concentrate my mind on what might be happening. I have to consider what else it is, if it's not bird flu.'

'You—' Beth began to speak then realised she didn't have the words she needed, so stared at him instead, disbelief vying with anger.

Anger won and she began again.

'You stalk out of my place, angry because one of us happened to have enough common sense to think about unwanted pregnancies, then come up here to sit beside a child you don't even know. I know I never understood you, Angus, but you sure as hell never understood me either.'

His turn to frown.

'What do you mean?'

Don't sigh! Stay mad!

But mad—angry mad—was something Beth found difficult to sustain, though she did swallow the sigh.

'I didn't stop tonight because of my so-called obsession about not having another child,' she said, hoping she was speaking crisply so he'd realise how maturely she was handling this argument. 'I stopped because I didn't want us back where we were before, with me being accidentally pregnant and you insisting on marrying me—of course you didn't *have* to but your moral code wouldn't allow otherwise. And for your information, I am *not* obsessed about not having another child.'

Angus was doing all right until she got to the 'not obsessed' part. That bit slipped beneath his skin.

Of course she had been. She'd gone ballistic—or as ballistic as Beth could ever go—when, after Bobby's death, he'd suggested it.

'Wasn't that why we parted?' he asked, aware he was treading in the dark and wondering what hidden traps might lie beneath his stumbling feet. 'So, if I wanted a child or children, I could have them with someone else? That's what you said.'

She shook her head—slowly—as if it was very, very heavy. Were her thoughts making it that way?

'We lived on different planets, didn't we?' she said, a note of deep regret in her voice. 'Together but apart because we couldn't understand each other's language. Not that we used language all that often.'

'We talked all the time,' Angus protested, although he knew they were empty words even before Beth raised her eyebrows. They *had* talked but never, ever about emotions.

'Anyway,' she said, sounding ridiculously cheerful and totally unconcerned about their coitus interruptus earlier, 'all that's in the past and it's probably just as well we didn't make love. We'd have ended up having a purely physical affair without giving it a moment's rational thought. Gone into it for all the wrong reasons!'

He stared at her, uncertain that this self-possessed woman, chatting easily and unemotionally about their shared past and purely physical affairs, could possibly be his Beth.

Though that Beth *was* his, he had no doubt! He didn't mean it in a possessive, ownership kind of way but since they'd met again—was it only last night?—he'd felt a deep certainty that they were meant to be together.

And always had been…

Though he could hardly say that now.

He replayed her last comments in his head and found something they *could* talk about.

'Are there wrong and right reasons for an affair where physical attraction is concerned?' he asked, and waited, keen to see just how this new Beth would respond.

She left her position in the doorway, where flight had probably been an option, and sat down beside him in the second chair, her hand reaching out to rest on Robbie's thigh.

'Of course there are,' she said, stroking the child's skin.

As an excuse for not looking at her ex-husband? 'A purely physical affair would be fine if both parties knew and accepted that's all it was—physical pleasure given and received. But if there were doubts, if both parties weren't in agreement or if the outcome of it—the parameters—were never discussed, it's nothing short of dangerous.'

'Experience talking, Beth?' he asked, because he couldn't help himself, though he regretted it the moment she looked up at him, hurt in her eyes.

'My only experience was with you, Angus,' she said quietly. 'So, yes, in a way it *is* experience talking. I know I went into our relationship thinking that's all it was—an affair—and though we didn't talk about it—we've been there, to the not talking, haven't we?—I assumed that's what you thought it would be as well. Two people attracted to each other, enjoying the attraction. We came from such different worlds I couldn't see how it would be otherwise. My pregnancy…' She shrugged. 'Well, who knows what might have happened?'

She'd turned away again, her eyes now fixed on the child. Which was probably just as well, because Angus had no idea what to say—what to reply—or even if a reply was necessary. She'd been right about them being on different planets—that's how it had been when Bobby had died—and that's exactly how he felt now, unable to put into words what he'd felt when he and Beth had begun their affair, unable to remember anything but the need he'd felt to be with her, and the strange melancholy that had followed him around whenever he hadn't been…

'Oh, you *are* here, Beth!' Marcia appeared in the doorway. 'Charles said to tell you, if you were still around, that Lily's conscious and quite lucid. Dreadfully tired and drawn but talking to him and Jill, asking about the bulls, would you believe?'

'That's great news,' Beth responded. 'And with Jack shifted back to a cabin in the camp you have to wonder if perhaps we've raised alarms too early. The two adults were okay earlier when I checked, although little Danny is still quite ill.'

'There's no such thing as too early with a situation like this,' Angus said, happy to switch from muddled emotional thoughts of the past to problems of the present. Problems he could deal with, but emotion—that was a different beast altogether. 'With only one or two people sick plus dead birds, it might have seemed alarmist, but you had five ill, now six, some seriously. No, it was right to put the wheels in motion for quarantine and further investigation.'

'So the mobile lab and decontamination unit will still come tomorrow?' Beth asked, then glanced at the clock on the wall. 'Or today, as it is now?'

'They will,' Angus said. 'Something has been making people sick and if it isn't the birds, what is it? Plus we've got to find out why the birds are dying. It's not as if it's one or two birds. I met a man called Grubby today and he had a bagful.'

'Trust Grubby to be involved,' Marcia said. 'And I bet he wasn't wearing gloves and a mask.'

'He wasn't, but his theory was interesting and I've put in a call to some bird experts on the mainland to see if there's some way we can test it.'

'Not until the containment lab arrives,' Beth said,

annoyed that she should feel such a clutch of panic at the thought of Angus in danger, yet unable to stop it.

So much for maturity! Not to mention parameters!

'That'll be exciting, won't it?' Marcia said. 'Like stuff you see on television when someone sends some white powder through the post and everyone thinks it might be anthrax.'

'I'm not sure "exciting" is the word I'd use,' Beth said. 'Look at Robbie here—he's not excited and neither's his mum, I bet.'

'Oh, she's okay now. I spoke to her tonight and told her the other little boy was already better and that Lily was over the worst and Robbie was resting more easily. I suppose she's so used to him being sick she doesn't get too stressed.'

Had Angus guessed what Beth had been about to say—that she was about to tell Marcia just how stressful every minor ailment or illness was for parents of a child with a disability—that he put his hand on her shoulder?

'He does seem to be doing better,' he said quietly.

And now that Beth turned her attention—all of it—from Angus to the child in the bed, she realised Marcia and Angus were right—Robbie did seem to be sleeping more naturally.

'So you don't need to sit here all night,' Marcia said. 'Either of you,' she added with a smile. 'I'll call you, Beth, if he becomes fretful.'

She disappeared but not before she'd smiled again—a knowing kind of smile that should have made Beth angry but instead made her feel sad.

But only for a moment. Kissing Angus had reminded

her of how good love-making had been between them, and had reminded her body of its needs. Not only reminding her but leaving her aching for the kind of bliss only Angus could bring to it.

Would it hurt to experience it again?

Surely not!

But could she make love with Angus without him realising how much she still loved him?

Of course she could! Hadn't she concealed her love from him throughout their marriage? Hadn't she held back from saying the words she'd longed to say because she'd known how awkward—how unwelcome—he'd have found them?

And wasn't she so much more mature now? Better able to handle such things?

Besides, wouldn't an affair—purely physical, of course—with Angus be a better memory to carry with her into the future than the memory of devastation she'd been left with when they'd parted?

Half-appalled yet totally excited by her thoughts, she took a deep breath and plunged into speech.

'Do you want to come back to my place?' she said, turning to the man she'd been so very angry with only a little earlier.

'Are you crazy?' Angus growled, keeping his voice low so he didn't disturb the sleeping child but still conveying his outrage. 'For what? So we can almost make love again?'

Beth shrugged, took a deep, silent breath, crossed her fingers for luck—or whatever—and said, as calmly as she could, 'More so you could spend what's left of the night there and be closer to the medical centre in the morning.

After all, that was your original idea. And it needn't be *almost* if we make love again, Angus.' Was her voice wavering? Was her trepidation obvious? Keep calm! Just say it. 'I'm the boss of this place. I know where they keep condoms.'

Angus stared at her, sure he should be offended by what she was saying yet so stunned to hear such words coming from shy, unworldly Beth he found them difficult to take in.

'You've just been talking about all the wrong reasons for going into an affair,' he muttered at her. 'Isn't this a prime example of a wrong reason—leftover lust from our marriage?'

To his surprise she smiled, although he suspected the smile didn't reach her eyes.

'I thought it was a prime example of the right kind of affair—no strings attached, like a holiday romance. We're talking about it first, so it's not just impulse. We both know it has no future because you'll be gone when the conference is over or the quarantine lifted and I'll be staying here. Perfect!'

Angus realised he didn't have a clue how to react. His body told him one thing—urging him to agree with Beth's invitation and analysis of the situation—while his mind was quite sure this wasn't Beth at all, just someone else in Beth's body—that delectable, sexy, desirable and utterly tantalising body. Though that last bit was his body talking again…

He opened his mouth then realised he was about to launch into a string of incomplete sentences, things like 'You' and 'I' and 'We'. Not even sentences, just pronouns, with no words to follow them because he had no idea what he wanted to say.

'It's up to you,' Beth said cheerfully, though he suspected he could hear a note of strain beneath the words. Was this all an act, this grown-up, independent, affair-discussing Beth? 'If you want to go back to the resort, I'll drive you back, but you decide. I'll meet you out front.'

And with that she disappeared.

To get some condoms?

The thought excited him—as did this new Beth, act or not! Not that she'd been dependent or clingy during their marriage, more that she'd been a follower—no, not even that. She'd just been there, willing to fit in—her upbringing leaving her with a need to please, but unobtrusively.

His chest tightened just thinking about it. The young foster-child, trying to be so good but invisible as well, hoping if she wasn't noticed, then she might be allowed to stay. He'd only met one of her foster-mothers, who'd explained she'd have been happy to keep Beth for ever, even adopt her, but Beth's maternal grandmother had been her guardian and she'd refused to release the child for adoption, or give her up completely, descending on whatever home Beth might be in to take her for a short time before tiring of the role of mother and giving her back to Children's Services.

Her grandmother, the only relation she'd ever known, had died shortly before he'd met Beth, and though Angus thought the woman had behaved very badly as far as Beth was concerned, Beth, in her gentle, trusting, accepting and unquestioning way, had loved her.

Were these thoughts helping his decision?

Of course not! They were making him even more confused, although if he accepted that the Beth who'd offered him a bed—and an affair—was a very different Beth to the one he'd married, surely that would make the affair okay.

He touched the sleeping child on the forehead, his mind sliding towards what-ifs.

Useless! This was here and now and Beth was offering him a chance at redemption. Oh, she might not know it. She might be thinking of a brief affair—although that suggestion was so foreign to the Beth he knew, he realised there was something he was missing—but he didn't have to agree to that. He didn't have to fit into her so-called parameters.

Did he?

He bent and kissed the little boy on the cheek, hoping somewhere in his sleep he might feel the caress, then he made his way to the front of the new building, night-quiet now the worst was over for the patients within it.

No, the little boy who'd had the seizure was still very ill and according to a doctor called Luke, who had been on duty when Angus had arrived, one of the adults from the resort wasn't much better, being monitored all the time, with respiratory support, fluids and non-steroidal anti-inflammatory drugs the only things they could give him until they knew exactly what had caused the illness.

Angus had heard the murmur of voices as he'd passed the man's room, and been reminded of just why he'd been called to the medical centre.

Not for an affair with his ex-wife, that was for sure, but until the lab arrived there was very little he could do.

Beth was sitting in the driving seat of one of the carts and Angus felt panic clutch at his intestines.

She'd changed her mind—

'I thought you'd need clean clothes, to say nothing of a razor and toothbrush, so I'd drive you over to the resort and you can either stay there or get your things and come back to my place. Up to you.'

Angus got warily into the cart and peered at the woman beside him, visible in the light of the moon they'd intended walking under earlier.

Was there a packet of condoms in her shorts pocket?

Excitement tightened his body and he peered at her again.

She looked like Beth, and her voice sounded the same, it was just—

He had no idea what it was, but it was time to find out. People didn't change this much for no reason and for all she'd said he was the only man she'd had in her life, he was beginning to suspect that might not be true. Someone or something had changed her in some way.

'I'll get my things and come back to your place,' he said, watching closely so he could read her reaction.

Except he couldn't—not even when she'd glanced his way before she started the cart. She steered them onto the narrow track that led into the rainforest, reaching into the shelf below the dashboard and handing him insect repellent.

'Put this on your face and arms. The mossies in the forest could carry you away they're so fierce.'

He took the cream and smoothed it on his skin, hating the smell of it but not wanting to be bitten.

They drove through the dark rainforest, aware from the wailing cries of the shearwaters, the buzzing of insects and the rustling movements in the ferns that the forest was as alive at night as it was during the day.

'The canopy made up of vines and plants—like staghorns and elkhorns that live high up in the trees—blocks out the moonlight, that's why it's so dark,' Beth said, needing to break the silence that was like a glass wall between them. 'Farther into the park, on the edge of the mountain, the park rangers have built a suspension walkway through the canopy, so you can see all the life that's up there.'

Angus remained silent and she began to wonder what on earth she'd done, asking him back to her place, suggesting he stay—a packet of condoms burning a hole in her pocket…

All to satisfy her lust?

She hoped she could pass it off as that, but in her heart of hearts she knew it wasn't anything to do with lust. What she wanted was some more time with Angus—a little period of togetherness she could enjoy then wrap up like a parcel and tuck away inside her, to be taken out and relived when she felt lonely or depressed.

Like a diamond tucked away somewhere safe, brought out to shimmer in the light from time to time. Better by far a memory like that than the bleak, black stone that had been Bobby's death and the harsh words she and Angus had exchanged so soon after it, before they'd each retreated into their separate cocoons of grief…

She stopped the cart where she'd parked it the previous morning, suddenly aware of just how long this day had been.

How confusing…

Would Angus go into the hotel and return or was he already regretting his earlier decision?

'Walk in with me?' he said, and Beth's heart leapt because she knew it meant he would return. Then she glanced down at the shorts and shirt she wore and decided walking through the lobby of a five-star resort in this attire wouldn't be the done thing, no matter how late the hour.

Or possibly *because* of the late hour.

'I'll wait here,' she said, and the wall crumbled, Angus leaning right through it to put his hand behind her head and draw it towards him, kissing her with such fierce urgency that desire flooded through her body.

'See that you do,' he said, then he was gone, striding along the path, past the ocean-like swimming pool and up the stairs into the foyer.

Her mobile chirped at exactly the moment Angus reappeared, small overnight bag in hand. Beth answered it, knowing it would be a summons to the hospital.

'The restful sleep didn't last long—can you come?' Marcia said, and Beth knew she would.

Angus saw the mobile held to her ear and asked a silent question.

She nodded in reply, her body tight with tension.

Would he turn and walk away?

Was that it?

The death of the diamond before she'd had it in her hand?

But he threw his bag into the back of the cart and climbed in beside her.

'If it's all right with you—' he began, and Beth, her heart too full for speech, just nodded in reply.

* * *

'You had the chance to go back to the hotel and didn't take it,' Angus muttered to himself as he dried himself, post-shower, in Beth's small bathroom.

He tried to analyse his irritation, deciding in the end it wasn't that Beth wasn't there, but that she *was* so much there in the little cabin she called a home. The soap he'd used in the shower and which had now scented his skin was the smell of Beth, the moss-green mosquito net he was unknotting from above the bed smelt like the little tea candles she'd sometimes lit in their bedroom, a romantic notion he'd looked upon indulgently but had fiercely missed when she had left.

And the bed, with its mountain of pillows and cushions of every size and colour, things he'd flung to the floor before sharing the bed in her little flat, then appreciated when she'd tucked them behind his back in the morning so he could sit and sip the cup of tea she always brought him.

Hell! He must have been the most spoilt, pandered to, pampered and unappreciative mongrel on earth, the way he'd let Beth look after him.

He climbed beneath the net, shifted a million cushions, then settled his head on a pillow.

Which smelt of her shampoo…

He sighed and, accepting the inevitable, breathed it in and, for the first time in three long years, slid peacefully into sleep.

CHAPTER SEVEN

ROBBIE was more than restless, he was crying, uttering little whimpering words that didn't make sense, and twisting in the bed as if his body was racked with pain.

Charles, looking grey and tired, was in the room when Beth entered, close by the bed, talking quietly to Robbie.

'Perhaps we did the wrong thing with the quarantine,' he said to Beth, when the little boy's spasms ceased and he seemed to sleep again. 'We could have airlifted Robbie and Mr Todd, the guest who's in a bad way, across to the mainland.'

'And done what there?' Beth queried.

Charles looked at her and shook his head.

'Watched them both, as we're doing here,' he admitted. 'Control the fluid intake so we're not adding to the pressure on the brain, control seizures with anti-convulsant medication—not that either of them have had seizures—monitor breathing, pulse and oxygen levels in the blood, measure urine output and test it for anomalies. That's what's really bothering me, Beth, the fact that with all our specialised medical knowledge there's nothing more we could be doing for these people on the mainland than we are here.'

He offered her a rueful smile.

'Yet I still feel guilty that they're here. Crazy, isn't it?'

'Not really,' she said. 'We've come to think we can work miracles with machines and drugs. We can put new hearts into tiny babies, even operate on them in the womb, we understand how the human body works and most of the diseases that afflict it, but we're not infallible, and neither is modern medicine. Like doctors always have, we just do what we can.'

His smile this time was even more strained.

'That's true of most things in life, I suppose,' he said quietly, then he wheeled backwards, leaving room for Beth to slip into the chair beside Robbie's bed and take his hand, talking quietly to him, hoping somewhere in his consciousness he'd know she was there and be soothed by her presence.

She was asleep, her head resting on the bed, her two hands clasping one of Robbie's. Angus stood and looked at her for a moment, seeing the shadows of tiredness beneath her eyes, the tangles in the silky dark hair.

He'd slept so well himself, wrapped in the scent of Beth, that he felt guilty, seeing her exhaustion. Not that she'd have slept in her own bed while she was worried about the child.

Although Robbie looked at peace again this morning, his breathing deep and easy. Hopefully, the crisis had passed and he was on the mend. Two of the other children had recovered quickly—well, not fully recovered, they were both tired and listless and would need careful watching for a week or two, but they were certainly well enough to leave the hospital.

Perhaps it was good the quarantine was in place, for with the number of hospital and camp staff and volunteers available it would be easier to keep Robbie on the island while he recuperated rather than sending him home to a harassed mother with four other children.

Children!

He frowned at the memory the word threw up. Last night Beth had denied she was obsessed about not having more children, yet surely the argument they'd had—the only real argument he could remember having with Beth—had been over having another child. He'd been trying to comfort her after Bobby's death and had said there'd be other children and she'd flown at him like a demented banshee—or were all banshees demented?

Anyway, they'd argued, then retreated into their separate cones of silence, held there by some misunderstanding, Angus had felt, as well as grief.

He studied Beth for a moment longer. Fate—and Robbie's setback—had kept them apart last night. If they'd come together, would they have talked?

Really talked?

He shook his head in rueful denial—they'd have made love all night, revelling in the pleasure they could bring to each other. Damn, his body was stirring just thinking about it.

He walked into the room, wondering if he should wake Beth, then walked out again, deciding she needed sleep more than she needed the confusing presence of her ex-husband.

Or he imagined she did, although now he'd realised he didn't know this Beth for all she looked and smelled the same. He wasn't sure what she might or might not need…

'We've had word from AQIS that the two mobile units will be in Crocodile Creek by midday and the army has one of their huge helicopters standing by to airlift them straight to the island.'

A tall man who introduced himself as Cal Jamieson was behind the desk in the office that had become, to Angus, the headquarters of the quarantine.

'I've persuaded Charles to go back to his cabin and get some sleep,' Cal continued to explain. 'This emergency, on top of Lily being sick, has really knocked him.'

'How is Lily?' Angus asked. He'd met the little girl on his first visit yesterday.

Cal smiled.

'Being difficult, would you believe? And "difficult" is a word we've never associated with Lily. She can be naughty, like all kids, but usually she's the most biddable child imaginable. Not this morning, though. She's sitting up in bed like an imperious little duchess, demanding to go home. When Gina, my wife, who was sitting with her, explained that no one could leave the island, she announced she didn't want to leave the island, she just wanted to go home to Jill and Charles because they were her new mummy and daddy and that's where she should be.'

'New mummy and daddy?' Angus queried.

But the phone rang and as Cal reached out to lift the receiver, he said, 'Ask Beth, she'll explain,' before adding a polite, 'Wallaby Island Medical Centre, Cal Jamieson speaking,' to whoever it was on the other end.

At a loose end, Angus mooched around the building, checked Beth was still asleep, then walked outside, slapping at a mosquito as he went, wondering if all the carts had insect repellent in them.

He found some in the first one he checked, and smoothed it onto his skin, noting as he did so it was a sun-screen factor 30 as well.

The mosquito he'd slapped at and missed buzzed around his head, but something else was buzzing inside it.

He walked back inside and found Cal was off the phone.

'What were the original symptoms of the illness?' he asked, and Cal frowned at him.

'Beth could probably list them straight off. I wasn't here when it began—not at the hospital—but from what I know, it was listlessness, a general malaise, achy feelings, headache, some vomiting.'

'Not flu symptoms?' Angus persisted.

'There must have been,' Cal said, 'because we talked of some kind of flu-like virus. I suppose general achiness is often an early symptom of flu—that might have been what set us on that path. Or, with the kids with lung problems, any illness at all is usually accompanied by chest infections. I know Susie, our physio, was involved from the start.'

He paused, studying Angus as if to read his thoughts.

Gave up and asked, 'What are you thinking?'

Angus waved the question aside.

'It's too vague even to be considered a thought at the moment, but my computer's back at Beth's place—I need to check out some stuff. The mosquitoes here—they're fresh-water?'

Now Cal looked downright puzzled.

'I guess they must be—aren't all mosquitoes? This far north we have a long wet season over summer each year and the rainforest is full of places where water can pool or puddle and mosquitoes can breed.'

'And you're how far from the mainland?'

'A half-hour helicopter flight, two hours by fast catamaran—about a hundred k's, I suppose.'

'That's far enough,' Angus said, more to himself than to Cal, thinking if what he suspected proved right, the virus wouldn't spread to the mainland.

Though how had it got to this island?

Thank heavens the island had wireless Internet connection facilities. Back at Beth's cabin, he brought his computer out to the deck table and booted it up, then tracked through all the sites he could find on mosquitoes. Japanese encephalitis was well known—there was even a vaccine available for people travelling to Japan or nearby Asian countries. The disease caused fever, headaches, vomiting and confusion, and there was no antiviral available. All specialists advised was to treat the symptoms.

Next he worked out how far they were from Japan—although the virus had also been found in Southeast Asia. Thousands of kilometres, but tracing the path mosquitoes would take he crossed the big island of New Guinea.

Vague memories surfaced—the miscellaneous file in his head again. The early days of colonisation in New Guinea—people suffering from some form of sleeping sickness. But malaria had raged there and the emphasis had been on finding drugs to deal with that. The sleeping sickness had stayed vague, more a myth than something written up in medical journals.

He switched his research to mosquitoes.

'The problem is,' he said to Beth who'd appeared, a sleep crease in her right cheek, at the bottom of the steps, 'that mosquitoes rarely travel more than a few hundred yards in their lifetimes, maybe a mile, unless, of course, there's wind assistance. But if they breed in the rainforest here, there's no wind—or virtually none…'

He stared at her as he tried to take his thoughts further.

Tired as she was, Beth felt warmth stirring inside her. A different warmth—remembered warmth—the kind she'd always felt when Angus had discussed things with her, using her as a sounding board for his thoughts.

Not that it meant anything to him—he simply found it easier to arrange his thoughts by talking through them. Probably Garf would have done just as well.

'And good morning to you, too,' she said, as she came up the steps, suddenly aware how daggy and sleep-rumpled she must look. 'Have you had breakfast? Would you like a cup of tea?'

The ordinary questions, far removed from how far mosquitoes might or might not travel, seemed to bring him out of his head.

'You sit, I'll get it. I found my way around your kitchen earlier. Went up to the hospital as well. You were sleeping so I didn't disturb you.'

The idea of Angus finding his way around her kitchen was disturbing somehow, although she'd asked him to come—to stay.

But if he could behave as if all this was perfectly normal, so could she. 'How is Robbie today?'

'Sleeping peacefully, but we thought he was over it when he was like that yesterday, so who knows? But Danny is still very ill. They've called in Alex Vavunis, the paediatric neurosurgeon, again.'

She felt the weight of the sick children bearing down on her again and must have shown her feelings, for Angus stood up and came towards her, wrapping his arms around her and giving her a comforting hug.

At least, she thought it was a comforting hug, for all it went on a tad longer than most hugs of that kind.

And reminded her of the packet of condoms in her pocket!

Hell's teeth! Had she really suggested an affair to Angus? Talked calmly about affairs and getting condoms?

Lack of sleep—that was the only possible reason she could find for such bizarre behaviour.

Although—she snuggled into the hug—was it such a bad idea or was it just the daylight making the condoms feel heavy and…tawdry, cheap in her pocket?

'Sit down, I'll get the tea,' he said, condoms obviously the furthest thing from his mind. 'And some cereal?'

She shook her head for cereal but did sit, mainly to get out of the hug. But as soon as Angus walked inside, she stood up and followed, aware how grubby and sleep-stupid she was feeling, needing a shower and clean clothes.

Needing to get rid of the condoms.

Or she could leave them in her shorts pocket in the laundry bin.

Mosquitoes. Focus on mosquitoes—better by far than focussing on Angus.

They'd been bad this year, worse, the rangers said, than previous years, and all island staff and visitors were advised to wear repellent at all times.

Showering quickly, she wrapped a sarong around her body, as she usually did on days off, and brought her thoughts into the kitchen where Angus was making toast, the possible lover of the previous evening having given way to the man of action.

'The camp kids have made a couple of trips into the forest at night—spotlighting. That's what we were doing when Sam spotted you and thought you were a Yowie.'

'And that's when the mossies are at their worst?' Angus said, spreading butter and strawberry jam on the toast then slicing it into fingers.

Beth nodded and smiled to think he'd picked up on her conversation so easily—the warm feeling back inside her.

'So the next thing is a visit to the ranger station,' he said. 'Tea and toast, then you might show me where to go.'

He raised an eyebrow and she nodded, though she'd have to change into sensible clothes. It wouldn't do to be traipsing around the island in a sarong and nothing else.

Although it seemed a shame…

The thought deserved a slapped cheek. How could she possibly be thinking of dallying with Angus when all the people on the island could be at risk of some unknown virus? The familiar throbbing grumble of a helicopter circling overhead again was a further reminder of how serious things were.

'Honestly,' she muttered, 'they're worse than the mossies!'

Then she took a finger of toast back into her bedroom,

eating it as she changed into very proper and practical shorts and a T-shirt.

Clean shorts—no condoms in the pocket—sensible, practical Beth once again.

'We'll take a cart,' she said, when tea and toast were finished and she was walking with Angus back towards the hospital.

But they were no sooner in the cart, when Garf joined them, forcing Angus to move closer to Beth.

'Oh, dear, you really shouldn't come, Garf! How did you get free?' Beth said helplessly to the dog, who was behaving as if he hadn't seen her for a month and was so delighted he might actually turn inside out with glee.

Garf stood on Angus's knee so he could lick Beth's cheek and she gave in.

'All right, but you'll have to stay in the cart,' she warned him sternly.

'Is the whole island a national park?' Angus asked as they drove into the rainforest.

'Technically, no,' Beth said. 'There's been a camp-type of resort at our end for over a hundred years. It started when there was a mutton-bird factory here—making oil—and people used to come over from the mainland to camp. Then some bright person saw a way of making money out of more than campers and built a resort at the other end. When the whole of the Great Barrier Reef was declared a national park, the waters around the island became a national park and not long after that the state government declared the state-owned land in the middle a dedicated park as well. The kids' camp and eco-cabins at our end and the resort at the other end are there on sufferance but what's the use of having pristine rainforest and stunning coral reefs if people can't come to experience and enjoy them all?'

'So Garf can legally live and play at either end of the island but not the middle bit?' Angus said, and the dog, hearing his name, gave him a lick as well.

'That's about it,' Beth agreed, turning onto the narrow track that lead to the ranger headquarters. 'And if he's out of the camp and hospital grounds, right now we're supposed to have him under strict control to keep him away from the dead birds. Last time I saw him he was tied up on the hospital veranda, which is where he's supposed to be. Wicked dog!'

But as she turned she caught a glimpse of white in the jungle-like growth to the side of the track and stopped.

'That must be one of the rangers there,' she said, pointing to where the suited figure had been. 'Let's stop and see if he's finding many dead birds.'

But before they could approach the tree which she was sure must hide the man in the white suit, he broke from cover and plunged into the undergrowth.

Beth made to follow, but Garf, sensing a bit of fun, leapt from the cart and gave chase, barking furiously.

'Hell! Now he'll really be in trouble!' Beth said. She yelled at the dog, who, trained to obey instantly, immediately turned back towards her, although the look he gave her was full of reproach.

'Get in the cart, you bad dog!' Beth ordered, not falling for the soulful-eyes routine.

But when she turned to Angus she was frowning.

'Why did he run?' she said, a shiver of apprehension travelling up and down her spine.

'Scared of dogs?' Angus suggested, but Beth shook her head.

'He ran before Garf chased him,' she pointed out. 'Let's go. Maybe someone at the station can tell us.'

But no one there could shed light on the mystery figure.

'My men and women are working around the perimeter of the park boundary because that's the most likely place the visitors would come in contact with the dead birds. They'll work inwards from there, but I've only six staff available and it will take them a couple of days to get in as far as where you saw the person in white.'

Angus had his own suspicions about the figure but there was no point in worrying either the head ranger or Beth. Besides, he was there for information.

'What types of mosquitoes do you have here?' he asked, and the ranger took them into his office and pulled down a thin book.

'It's years since we've had a specialist entomologist here, but these were the ones discovered last time a survey was done.'

He opened the book, showing illustrations and Latin names of a number of mosquitoes.

'Their family name is *Culicidae*, then the genera comes after that—*Anopheles* is the most well known because it carries malaria in areas where it is still endemic, but we have aedes and culex varieties as well. You're thinking?'

'If it's not the birds, then some kind of arbovirus,' Angus told him. 'These are spreading, and more and more cases of viral encephalitis are now being connected to mosquito carriers. In the United States you have West and East equine encephalitis that can both affect humans, and West Nile virus, then there's La Crosse, which is fairly new in the US as well, affecting mainly children, and Chikungunya fever, first isolated in Tanzania but now found throughout Africa and Asia. At first it was thought *Aëdes aegypti* was the only carrier, but they've now discovered that *Aëdes albopictus* could carry it, and you've that little fellow right here.'

He pointed to a mosquito illustration, running his finger down the abdomen.

'Pointed abdomen with pale bands basally—that's him.'

'And Chika-whatever means?' Pat, the ranger, asked.

'It's a debilitating illness with fever, headache, nausea, muscle and joint pain, and although patients recover quite quickly, it can leave its victims with feelings of listlessness and fatigue. I'm not saying that's what we've got here, but the illness could be a new variant of an arboviral encephalitis.'

'But why now?' Beth asked. 'I imagine there have always been mosquitoes on the island—why now would people be getting sick?'

'Driving along the track, from the resort to the medical centre, and then to this place, I've seen a number of huge trees that were obviously damaged during the cyclone that destroyed the original medical centre. Where they've been uprooted, you get depressions in the ground that fill with water and make ideal breeding grounds. And the cyclone gives us another clue. From the quick research I did before coming here, I know most of these virus-carrying mosquitoes are already prevalent in Asia and in a number of Pacific Islands. And in New Guinea, not that far to the north, there have always been arboviral illnesses—malaria and dengue being the most common. So, what if the cyclone blew some new mosquito strains this far—mosquitoes carrying a known or unknown viral encephalitis?'

'And these have bred and now people who haven't been wearing protective clothing or repellent have been bitten and the virus passed on to them?' Beth whispered.

'It makes sense.'

'Are you saying it's definitely not bird flu?' Pat asked, and Angus shook his head.

'We don't know. I've just been exploring other ideas—thinking out loud, really. The lab arrives this afternoon. With luck I'll be able to test some blood from the dead birds and either confirm or eliminate avian influenza from the equation. The fact that the sick children are showing signs of recovery gives me some hope that it's not—or not H5N1 because that has shown itself to be deadly.'

'So my people keep collecting dead birds?'

Angus nodded.

'It's in your interest to collect them anyway, I would think. If there is something wrong with them—some illness—you wouldn't want other predatory birds feeding on them and getting ill themselves.'

'Good grief, no!' Pat muttered, as if this was the first time he'd thought further than the collection stage of this operation. 'And on top of that, we've got your mystery person in the undergrowth.'

He frowned then said, 'Perhaps it *was* one of my staff,

who moved away because he or she knew it wasn't the right place to be.'

'Or an intrepid reporter,' Angus suggested. 'There've been helicopters buzzing overhead—how easy would it be for one of them to land someone on the far side of the island?'

'But would someone risk it?' Beth asked. 'Risk coming to a place where they could be infected by a potentially life-threatening illness?'

'The person was suited up and probably masked,' Angus reminded her, then he smiled. 'Though I doubt he'd get much of an interview dressed like that.'

'A photographer could still take photos while wearing a mask. If he takes photos of dead birds, perhaps people coming and going at the medical centre, the arrival of the mobile labs—wouldn't that be enough for front-page news?' Beth asked, adding, 'As far as I can see, they make up most of the stories that go with photos.'

Angus nodded.

'Photos are much more emotive—think how distressed the families of people on the island will be when they see them. We'll have to find the man.'

'Or woman,' Pat reminded him. 'But how? And is it such a worry? We've got the local paper reporter here already and surely people are already sending photos from their mobile phones.'

'They're always blurred,' Angus pointed out. 'And probably the only people with mobile phones who'd do that are guests at the resort and, believe me, they'd be hard pushed finding a piece of gravel out of place on the paths, let alone a dead bird. No, I can see a newspaper editor wanting photos—maybe even video footage for a television broadcast. The policeman, Beth—what's his name?'

'Harry Blake. He'll be in one of the staff cabins. Grace is on duty this week.'

'Let's find him. And, Pat, tell your rangers to keep an eye out but also remind them about insect repellent. And you might start thinking about mosquito-control measures we can safely take without endangering other animal or plant species in the national park.'

'Great!' Pat muttered. 'Mosquito control. Fish are the best because they eat the larva but that's long term and will only work in the pools of permanent water. Short term's usually poison of some kind and animals in the rainforest drink from the fresh-water holes and from water that collects in the dead palm fronds—we can't poison their water supply.'

'Get on the Net and see what you can find—there has to be some short-term solution,' Angus said. 'I realise it's by no means certain that what we've got is an arbovirus, but if it is we'll have the opportunity to wipe it out before it reaches the mainland. Remember that dengue was unknown there until recent years and look how far south that has spread.'

Pat nodded, said goodbye to Beth then turned to his computer.

'He's a good man,' Beth told Angus as they returned to the cart.

'A good man with a heap of worries on his shoulders,' Angus replied, ordering Garf to move over. 'I want to see out as we go,' he told the dog, who showed him a hurt face again—to no avail.

Angus wasn't looking for the stranger in the rainforest, but for pools of water where mosquito larvae could live.

'How long since it's rained?' he asked, as Beth drove them back towards the camp.

'Two weeks at least—we had a storm but it was well before the kids' camp started.'

'And there's still water lying in palm fronds,' he muttered, as much to himself as to Beth. 'If it's two weeks since you had rain then clearing the forest of water would be impossible. It's everywhere.'

'It's rainforest,' Beth reminded him, and he smiled because, bothered as he was by this viral outbreak, there was something very satisfying in being with Beth again, talking to her, sitting beside her as she competently guided the little cart through the forest. Even the dog made him happy.

'We could get a dog.'

The words had come out before he could stop them, and when he peered past Garf to get Beth's reaction, she was staring at him, eyes wide in disbelief.

'Angus,' she said, very carefully as if the word might burn her mouth. 'There is no we. You live in an apartment, and I already have a dog, or the use of one most of the time.'

She rested her head against Garf for an instant.

'Don't I, Garf?' she said, whispering now—sad, somehow…

She dropped Angus at the hospital where he had to check on the arrival of the mobile laboratories, tied Garf up again, then left the cart in the small parking area and walked home, wondering just how they'd managed to get into such an emotional muddle so quickly.

And it was 'they', not just her—Angus's remark about the dog had made that clear.

Was he, like she, thinking how comfortable it was, them being together?

Beth had to assume so but being comfortable together didn't mean much. Being comfortable together was fine in the good times but come the bad times, when that comfort disappeared, couples needed more.

They needed communication—talking-type communication, not just being good together in bed—and talking-type communication was difficult for both herself and Angus.

Although they could talk about mosquitoes, and arboviruses—it was emotional stuff they couldn't talk about. They couldn't even say 'I love you' to each other but, then, Angus didn't love her—never had…

Her thoughts made her feel ashamed of bringing home the condoms—worse, suggesting an affair with Angus.

For all she longed for that bright, shining diamond of memory, she really wasn't an affair kind of person—she'd known that the first time—and having an affair with Angus would only make her more unhappy when he left.

So?

'I've no idea,' she said to a tiny finch that had fluttered into the tree in front of her then flew to rest on the railing of her deck, leading her home, or so it seemed.

Maybe if she had a proper sleep she'd be able to think it through more clearly.

Maybe!

The pillow smelt of Angus and she wrapped her arms around it and breathed in the smell of him as she drifted into sleep.

CHAPTER EIGHT

VIBRATIONS shook Beth's cabin and a roaring noise made her wonder if a tsunami was about to hit the island, then the shuddering lessened and she realised what had woken her—the big army helicopter delivering a mobile lab for Angus.

She leapt out of bed but could see nothing. Of course not—the labs were to be landed on the mainland side of the island, far from the areas where children camped and tourists strayed.

But Angus would be there, ready, dead birds in hand, so to speak. He would also be testing blood from the victims, though he'd been grumbling that the tests he'd have available would take longer.

A quick shower, shorts and a T-shirt, sandals on her feet, and she was ready to go. He'd need a lab assistant and even if he didn't need one, he'd have one. If Angus was going to be in that chamber, testing things, she wanted to be right there with him.

Not because she had any silly ideas of danger, or romantic notions they should die together—Angus was far too careful to fall victim to the risks inherent in his work—

but because she knew that being there—someone being there—would make things easier for him. It would ease the tension that being in a small, sealed space would naturally bring, and having someone to talk to would help his thought processes.

She grabbed a cart outside the medical centre and drove on the rarely used track to the beach on the far side of the island. The helicopter had departed, leaving a silence that seemed heavy and threatening somehow.

'No bird noises,' she whispered to herself, praying it was because the competition of the helicopter's engines had silenced them, not because the entire bird population of the island was now dying. It was late afternoon, the time the birds were usually coming home, flying back in flocks from their day hunting out at sea.

Then the chattering began again and relief flooded through her. Her beautiful island was still alive.

Charles and Angus were sitting in a cart at the top of the beach, staring at the shiny white cube that had been deposited by the helicopter. Grubby was striding around it, as if searching for a way in, though perhaps he was simply seeing it was positioned safely.

'I'm sorry to leave you on your own here, but we've had to airlift young Danny to Brisbane and I've got to deal with the repercussions of breaking quarantine,' Charles was saying to Angus, who climbed out of the cart as Beth pulled up beside them. 'Beth? Have you come to look at the box that came from the sky?'

Beth smiled at the weak joke.

'I've come to help,' she announced. 'I may not be one hundred per cent up to date on pathology or lab techniques, but I do know most labs have lab assistants. So, one lab assistant, ready and available.'

Charles didn't answer for what seemed like a very long time.

'You don't have to do this.' His voice was low and very serious when he finally spoke. 'I wouldn't ask you to, and I certainly am not asking you to volunteer. Angus knows the risks involved in any situation like this, but you?'

'I'm volunteering without being asked,' Beth assured Charles, more concerned by the weariness in Charles's voice and the strain showing on his face than in the job she was about to undertake.

Not that she could do much, he was her boss and she barely knew him. What puzzled her was that if, as everyone was saying, Charles and Jill were about to marry, the imminent occasion didn't seem to be creating much joy in either of them.

Although she hadn't shown much joy or delight when she'd married Angus—she'd been distracted by feelings of fear and trepidation and a hefty dose of guilt.

She watched the little cart, with Charles in it, head back to the medical centre, and hoped he'd find the joy that seemed to be lacking in his life at the moment.

'You don't have to do this. I don't need anyone to assist.'

The cause of her old guilt was speaking to her in crisp, matter-of-fact Angus tones.

'No, but I can wash the test tubes for you or hold things or do whatever lab assistants do. That's why I came across.'

He studied her for a moment, then said, 'It's a controlled environment and I'll be properly suited. It's not at all dangerous, you know.'

She nodded.

'Of course not. That's why I'm happy to help.'

He looked at her again, then out to sea, towards the mainland, and she knew he was wanting to deny her help, but couldn't work out how to do it without admitting there could be an element of danger in what they were about to do.

'This is the bio-hazard lab. I've told them to hold off delivering the decontamination chamber. If I find it's not bird flu and there's no need for decontamination, we won't need it.'

'So, let's get started,' Beth said, nodding to Grubby who seemed satisfied the unit was sited safely and was now moving a bag of dead birds out of his cart, setting it down at the door of the unit.

Angus hesitated. He longed to tell her to go away, to tell her he didn't want her involved in what he was about to do, but he couldn't without admitting there could be a minuscule element of danger in the process of dissecting the dead birds and testing the blood of infected patients, and he knew her well enough to know she'd insist they share the danger.

So he'd just have to make sure he eliminated that minuscule risk.

'Okay,' he said. 'Inside the door there's a chamber with suits, air bottles and breathing masks. We dress in there, fit the masks, make sure everything's working, then move into another, smaller chamber. It's a positive pressure airlock so nothing from inside can get outside. We shut the outer door and the inner door won't open until the air pressure is right in the lock, then we go on into the lab. It has directed air flow that goes up through a series of filters in the ceiling which trap and hold all the gases given off. We're breathing air through our masks, air from the bottles, not the air in the lab. Do not remove your mask, your gloves or any other item of clothing, okay?'

Beth nodded, then she smiled.

'Not the place to start our affair, then,' she teased, and though he knew she'd said it to lighten the tension growing between them, it made him flinch. His body may be excited by the thought of the affair she'd suggested, but the part of his mind not totally focussed on the island's problems had been toying with the idea and he knew he didn't like it.

Didn't like the parameters…

Which was probably why he'd made the stupid suggestion about the dog…

'We'll talk about *that* later,' he growled, taking a key from the leather bag the helicopter had dropped and fitting it to the door of the unit.

It unlocked easily, and he slid in the bag Grubby had left, waited until Beth was inside, then followed, bringing with him the small cool-box with the patients' blood and sputum samples.

A light had come on as he opened the door and he knew the solar panels on the top of the unit had kept the batteries fully charged. From the information he'd received from the army earlier, these batteries would supply power for four hours, then a generator would kick in, supplying power for another four hours. But well before that, Grubby would have run leads across from the nearest electricity supply point on the island and they'd be on mains power.

They dressed in silence, then passed together through the airlock into the lab itself.

It was weird, Beth decided, to be shut in such a small space with someone you knew so intimately yet have no intimacy between them at all. They could have been robots—or was it the distortion of their voices as they spoke through the masks that made her think that way?

Angus had cut through three birds, talking all the time into a microphone above the lab counter, detailing his findings, making suppositions as he saw the wasted muscles on the birds—the way the dark red breast muscles had withered away from the breastbone—taking samples and passing them to Beth to seal and label.

That she was allowed to do, but he wouldn't let her touch the birds, insisting he drop them in the waste container, although he let her seal it when the final bird was set inside it. Neither was she allowed to clean the stainless-steel bench. Angus took care of it, wiping it with paper towels that went into a new waste container, then spraying a heavy duty anti-bacterial agent over it and wiping it again.

'Now bloods,' he said, moving to the opposite bench, examining the new, state-of-the-art machines arrayed there.

'Ah,' he said, the sound conveying satisfaction. 'We have the very best, the very latest—the MChip. It will still take a couple of hours for the tests to run, but with computerisation we won't get a false positive.'

He was busy preparing samples for testing, and Beth stood back, handing him things as he needed them, putting labels on samples when asked, aware he could be doing this on his own yet pleased to be near him.

Mainly pleased. His 'we'll talk about that later' remark still niggled in her head, disrupting her concentration from time to time, puzzling her, for what was there to talk about?

Although hadn't she been thinking they should talk about their feelings? Ho! She and Angus *talk*? That kind of talk? It was an impossible dream—

'Did you hear me?'

She shook her head, startled out of her thoughts.

'I said you should sit down, or you could go—there's really nothing to do.'

Angus waved his hand towards the machines, which were evidently doing whatever they were meant to do with his samples.

'You go out through that door.' He pointed to a door at the other end of the lab from the one they'd entered. 'There's another airlock chamber then a shower room. Strip off, put your gear into a drum and seal it, then shower and go through to the other side of the shower room and you'll find scrub suits.'

She saw his eyes gleam behind the protective glasses he was wearing.

'Hardly summer beach wear on an island but less bulky than our current garb. You look like a fat little caterpillar.'

He sounded gentle—loving—and although she knew it was probably the mask muffling his voice, not emotion at all, her bones felt melty and his name, 'Oh, Angus!', was little more than a sigh on her lips.

Gloved hands touched her shoulder and she stared at him—a tall white-suited figure, no bit of him visible except his eyes through glass. But his eyes seemed to be saying things to her—the eyes she'd never been able to read.

It was the glass, or maybe too much oxygen in the air mix she was breathing—of course Angus's eyes weren't saying that he loved her.

'I'll stay,' she said, holding his gaze, determined not to let him guess at her wild fancies. 'I want to know the results as much as you do.'

'They should have them by now on the mainland—the FluChip takes longer but it still gets there.'

'The samples were lost,' she said, wondering if anyone had told him that. 'It took a while to track them down.'

He nodded. 'And the spinal fluid samples came back negative for meningitis, and with a false positive for encephalitis.'

'False positive?' Beth echoed, both relieved and sorry they'd got back onto scientific talk.

'Something that looks like encephalitis but is unidentifiable as yet. They need to do more tests. The labs are still working on it.'

'It fits with your mosquito theory, doesn't it?' Beth said.

'Enough for Pat to have started putting mosquito traps around in the rainforest and to have asked for an entomologist to fly in as soon as the quarantine is lifted. He needs guidance on how to control them if it is a new arboviral encephalitis—or one that's new to Australia.'

Something beeped behind Angus and he turned away again, leaving Beth to wonder if she really did want to stay locked up with him for the next few hours.

The alternative, she realised, was sitting at home, wondering if he was all right, imagining the worst—he'd fallen and hit his head, run out of air and not realised it, both scenarios having him lying unconscious on the floor of the small lab.

Ridiculous, of course, but she'd accepted years ago that part of loving someone was imagining the worst.

She perched on the bench on the far side of the small room and watched the man she loved manipulating knobs and buttons, tapping information into the computer, feeding samples into machines, his hands sure and steady, as they'd been when they'd made love—as they'd been when he'd held Bobby…

Had she said she didn't want another child?

She was sure she hadn't, and tried to think back to that time of loss and grief and terrible loneliness.

'I didn't want a replacement for him,' she murmured, only realising she'd spoken her thoughts aloud when Angus turned towards her, eyebrows raised behind his protective glasses.

She shook her head and he turned away, hopefully deciding he'd heard her sigh, not speak. But as she dug deeper into her memories she began to realise how easily they could have picked up the wrong messages from each other.

Lack of communication again!

Now she did sigh, leaning her head back against the wall and letting the air come out softly.

'Okay!'

Startled out of her daze by the muffled word of triumph, Beth straightened up and looked across the room, to where Angus was pointing at a screen.

'See that?' he said, pointing at a pattern of dots on the screen. 'Now look at this.'

'This' was a totally different pattern of dots—luminescent dots.

'The second one is bird flu and our pattern definitely isn't that. In fact, it's not a flu virus at all, so we're back to mossies and encephalitis and although that can have severe consequences and debilitating effects, it's not the start of some pandemic. I'll still send the bird samples to the mainland and some whole birds, too. They can go back in the lab, so they're contained. But we're all done here, so let's go and tell folks the good news. Charles can raise the quarantine, people can leave the island—'

'Angus, it's ten o'clock. I doubt if anyone is sitting on a packed suitcase, waiting to leave the island, and hopefully Charles is sleeping. He's been looking terribly tired and stressed.'

Behind his mask she was sure Angus was smiling when he said, 'You're right about the general raising of the quarantine, but do you want to bet Charles isn't sitting outside the unit, waiting for a result?'

'I do hope he's not,' Beth said, anxious for the man who'd been so kind to her.

Angus was tidying things away, stacking vials into a small freezer.

'Does that run all the time?' she asked, relief that it wasn't bird flu allowing room to marvel at the equipment in the mobile laboratory.

'It has its own battery and inverter running off the solar panels with its own small generator to kick in if the batteries fail. But when mains power is on, that tops up the batteries as well, so this has fridge and freezer capacity all the time.'

He closed the door then nodded towards the exit, clearly marked.

'You go ahead and shower,' he said. 'I'll be a few minutes here.'

Which neatly saves any conversation about showering together, Beth thought, remembering his 'talk about it' statement once again.

She went ahead, stripping off her suit and the clothes underneath it, dropping the lot into bins to be taken away.

And no doubt destroyed, but she had other shorts and T-shirts. She showered, then dressed in a scrub suit and stepped out of the unit, finding Charles, as Angus had foretold, sitting in a cart at the top of the beach.

As she walked towards him a light flashed. Had Charles flashed his headlights?

Beth shook her head, too tired to think, although as she drew closer to the cart she smiled and called to Charles, telling him the good news. Behind her she heard the door of the unit close and a key turning in a lock—Angus.

'Angus will explain,' she told Charles, as another light flashed. 'Did you see the light? I guess it's one of the rangers, doing a spotlighting tour for resort guests.'

Charles made a noncommittal noise.

'Are you all right?' Beth asked, driven beyond boss and employee lines by the exhaustion in his face.

'Should I be?' he said wearily. 'We've had an outbreak of a potentially fatal disease on the island—and bird flu or encephalitis are both potentially fatal—I've had my ward—daughter—Lily in hospital, we've had to break the quarantine to fly a desperately ill child to the mainland, and now Susie's collapsed and she's in the medical centre, possibly with the same thing the others have had but Miranda thinks it's ARDS.'

'Oh, Charles, I'm sorry,' Beth managed, wanting to put her hand on his shoulder, to offer the comfort of touch. She knew from listening to the others talk how often Charles had helped or comforted them, but from whom did *he* draw his strength. From Jill?

Beth doubted that Jill had much to offer at the moment. She'd been looking tired and stressed herself the few times Beth had seen her recently.

'Do you want me back on duty at the centre?' she asked, thinking practical help was all she had to offer.

Charles offered her a tired smile.

'You've done enough,' he said. 'I know you're not the type to make a fuss, it's one of the reasons I wanted you for this job, but going into that lab today was a very brave thing to do, Beth. You wouldn't have been human if you hadn't had reservations.'

Beth shook her head. No need to admit she had had reservations—but they'd been more for Angus than for herself.

Angus joined them and Beth stepped aside, returning to the cart she'd driven to the beach. She was finished here. Charles and Angus could work out what happened next—as far as the quarantine and encephalitis was concerned.

What happened next with her and Angus—well, that was a different matter. She was starting to have qualms about her suggestion they have an affair…

* * *

Beth left the cart at the medical centre. Charles and Angus parked beside it, deep in plans. Inside the centre she looked into the room where Susie lay, Alex by her side. He nodded at Beth as if to say, *I have everything under control*, and she moved on to Robbie's room. He was sleeping, so there was nothing for her to do except to walk back through the bird calls of the night towards her hut.

But once inside, what? Crawl naked into bed? Would that look too needy?

And what the hell should she do with the condoms?

Forget about them?

Leave them on the shelf in the bathroom—where Angus couldn't help but see them?

Put them on the bedside table, within reach?

How stupid to be thinking such things. Angus must be exhausted—all he'd want to do was sleep, which was what she should be doing.

But if that's what he wanted, should she pull out the couch—make it up into a bed—at least leave sheets and pillows out?

She reached her hut—the home that had become a refuge—and, not knowing any answers, walked on to where the tide shushed against the coral sand, crystal clear, so she could see the small, flat sand sharks darting in the shallows. She walked into the water, up to her ankles, up to her knees, letting the warm moisture soak into the thin fabric of the scrub suit, then she turned and splashed along parallel to the beach, not wanting to get out, not wanting to go deeper, watching the water she kicked up arc into the air in tiny diamond drops.

Her diamond fantasy was ridiculous.

An affair with Angus would start the pain again—pain she'd barely learnt to erase from her life.

She could pretend she was mature enough to cope with it, probably pretend enough to fool Angus, but she couldn't fool herself.

'We're lifting the quarantine in the morning. I have to give my paper at the convention which means I won't be involved in meetings and press announcements, so I thought I might go back to the hotel and sleep.'

He'd come up behind her while she was splashing water at the silver streak of moonlight that lay across the lagoon.

Close behind her, but not touching.

And in spite of all the things she'd just decided, she heard herself saying, 'You could stay here.'

She didn't turn, though she heard him move, heard the water wash around his legs. Then his hands were on her shoulders and he was turning her towards him.

'Stay for an affair?' he whispered, looking down into her face, his own as unreadable as ever.

Stay for ever, Beth wanted to say—to yell it out loud so there could be no mistake.

But all she did was nod.

'I don't think that would suit me,' he said, then he bent his head and kissed her on the lips. 'Or you either, but I can only speak for myself, Beth.'

He kissed her again, harder this time, so her lips gave way and her mouth welcomed his tongue, taking it greedily inside, wanting more and more of him.

His hands slid around her back, holding her close, so there was no mistaking how his body felt about it.

She snuggled into him, sure all her doubts would be swept away if only—

No, don't think, just kiss. Kissing Angus, being kissed by Angus—was there any better feeling?

The kiss deepened and her thoughts strayed, muddled, drifting, lost in the heat and wonderment of sensation, in the building of excitement in her body. She felt herself trembling in his grasp, her nipples hurting as they pressed against his chest, an ache of wanting deep within her.

Then he wasn't there—cool air washing over her no doubt swollen lips—she could hear his voice but not make sense of what he was saying. Something about not wanting an affair, not liking her parameters, he'd see her, or maybe not, and wasn't it time she was in bed?

'Angus?'

She hated the sound of pleading in her voice but hadn't been able to prevent it.

'Now isn't the time to be talking,' he said, suddenly sounding as exhausted as she felt. 'But we will talk, Beth. Tomorrow I'll be busy in the morning. Later in the day?'

He held her elbow as she walked out of the water—polite to the last.

What was she supposed to say?

Should she suggest a time for them to 'talk'?

Like a dental appointment?

And what had he meant by not liking the parameters?

'We've *never* talked!' she muttered, anger coming to her rescue, pulling her out of the post-kissing daze and the no-affair shock. 'Not about emotional stuff!'

His smile raised the stakes as far as anger went, incensing her, but before she could react—or find a piece of driftwood and hit him really hard with it—he was speaking again.

'Not really. That's why we should, wouldn't you say?'

She opened her mouth to yell at him, though what she'd yell she didn't know, and while she dithered he stole the initiative again, closing her lips and blanking out her mind with one last kiss.

'Goodnight, Beth,' he murmured against her skin, then he turned her in the direction of her cabin and eased her gently in that direction.

Moving like an automaton, she went, one foot in front of the other, unable to think at all because she had no idea how to untangle what thoughts she had—where to start unwinding them so she could take a good look at them and try to work out what had happened.

Inside the living room she stripped off the scrub suit then made her way to the bathroom, where the packet of condoms mocked her from the laundry basket.

Muttering an oath she'd heard often but had never used before, she picked them up and flung them through the window. It was only as she climbed into bed, in her sensible pyjamas with sweet peas all over them, that she remembered the camp kids walked past that side of her hut to get to the art and pottery room so she had to get out of bed, find a torch and search through the undergrowth for the tell-tale packet.

Prickles spiked her bare feet and she cursed again as she fought the tangle of vines in the undergrowth, thinking now of snakes—night snakes—fear battling the need to find the darned packet.

She picked up a stick that had jabbed into her thigh and threw it deeper into the bushes. Then, out of nowhere, a yellow body hurled itself after the stick. Garf had escaped again and was sensing fun.

'Go away, you stupid dog,' Beth yelled at him, but Garf knew she loved him and ignored her anger, pouncing around in the bushes, then stilling suddenly, head alert, eyes on the darkness of the trees beyond the bushes.

But before Beth had time to wonder what Garf had sensed—please, heaven, it wasn't a snake—she spotted the packet.

There!

She darted forward and thrust her hand into the bushes, then stood up, clutching it, triumphant.

Garf grabbed at it, but she held on, hearing the cardboard tear as she scolded the dog.

'It's not a stick—let go!' she yelled, furious with him now, but he was having too much fun and he kept hold of his end of the small packet, shaking his head to dislodge her grip.

She was beginning to worry about the contents of the packet getting loose and choking him, when light flashed again, but this time there was a scuffling noise and Garf forgot the packet. He gave a sharp yap and dashed into the bushes while Beth wondered what on earth was happening.

She called the dog back, knowing he couldn't go chasing through the national park, but as he reluctantly returned to her side and she gathered up the spilt condoms—how many were supposed to be in the packet?—she wondered about the intruder. Maybe not a ranger spotlighting—maybe a peeping tom.

On the island?

Not with a flashlight!

She dismissed the thought. Kids mucking around with torches—there were a couple of young boys at the resort who'd been plaguing the camp kids. Probably bored with resort life and playing games over here…

She hurried back to her cabin and slipped the torn packet into her rubbish bin, covering it and its now useless contents with the discarded scrub suit.

Much to her surprise, given the tumult of the day, she slept deeply and well, waking in the morning and looking around at the bright sunshine, unable to believe she hadn't stirred.

'Emotional exhaustion!' she muttered to herself, as if she needed to excuse a good night's sleep. 'Not something Angus will be suffering from!'

Good. She still felt very peeved with Angus.

More than peeved—angry!

Hadn't he realised just how much inner strength it had taken for her to suggest an affair—how tongue-tyingly, gut-wrenchingly difficult she'd found it, not only to say the words but to sound so casual and worldly and—yes, mature—as she'd said them?

And he'd turned her down!

Didn't like the parameters—whatever that might mean!

Well, he could go to hell. She was over him. Seeing him again had been good because now she knew he wasn't interested in her she could move on to the next step of her life and find someone who was.

Or who might be…

The pain in her chest suggested she might be fooling herself, but she knew about pains. They faded in time.

They didn't disappear altogether, but they got manageable enough to be put away in a far corner and more or less ignored.

This one, too, would shrink.

Eventually…

'Dr Beth?'

Sam's voice.

'Come in,' she called, hopping out of bed and straightening her pyjamas so she was decently covered.

The little boy sidled across her living room, his face tight with worry.

She hurried to him, kneeling by his side and putting her arm around his skinny shoulders.

'What's wrong, love?'

He nestled against her.

'They took Danny away. They said he was too sick to stay, but Robbie's sick and he stayed. Did Danny die?'

'Oh, Sam, of course he didn't,' Beth assured him, lifting the child and sitting down so he was on her lap, her arms around him. 'It's just that they had to take special pictures of his head and we don't have the right machines here at the medical centre, so he went across to Crocodile Creek, where Bruce comes from, then down to Brisbane to a big hospital.'

Sam turned his head and his dark brown eyes looked steadfastly into her face.

'It's bad to tell lies to children,' he reminded her, and she hugged him as she smiled.

'It's not a lie, darling,' she whispered, rocking him in her arms, sadness flooding through her that a child so young should know so much about death and lies. 'Danny's sick, yes, but he had to go for scans—you know about scans. That's all. Actually, we heard last night that the scans were good—that the operation Stella's dad did on his head made him a whole lot better.'

Sam nodded his acceptance and snuggled closer to her, then changed the subject, reminding Beth how quickly children's moods could swing.

'CJ comes from Crocodile Creek,' he said, mentioning Cal and Gina Jamieson's little boy. 'And Lily. Lily's home now, in the cabin. Did you know?'

Beth agreed she did know, having heard about Lily's insistence on returning.

'She said she'd be my girlfriend.'

Beth had been thinking how fragile Lily had seemed and wondering if letting her out of hospital had been such a good idea, so it took a moment for Sam's words to sink in.

'Girlfriend?' she repeated helplessly. He was, what—eight?

'Like Stella is for Jamie,' Sam explained.

'Ah!' Beth murmured, as if understanding the girlfriend concept for the first time. Perhaps it was the first time—perhaps she'd never understood it any more than she understood relationships.

'I took a flower to her cabin,' Sam continued.

Beth smiled, although she was fairly sure she should be lecturing him on not picking flowers.

'And did she like it?'

'I don't know. The cabin was real quiet so I left it on the deck.'

'That was kind of you. Lily needs to sleep a lot so if she was sleeping, it was best not to wake her. Now, where are you supposed to be? Where are Benita and the other kids?'

'They're walking on the beach before breakfast. We walked up to the point then turned around, but I ran and got here first, because of the flower, you see.'

He'd no sooner explained than Beth heard the chatter of the children returning.

'I've got to get dressed and go over to see Robbie, so how about you join them and maybe after breakfast we can do something?'

'Not today,' Sam told her, recovered enough now to climb off her knee. 'We're going fishing. In a boat. I'm going to catch a king.'

'A king fish?' Beth guessed.

Sam shook his head.

'No. Some other kind of king—it's big and pink and I'll show it to you at lunchtime because we're coming back for lunch.'

And with that, he was gone, a little boy with a tenuous hold on life, but making every second of it count.

While she was wasting hers…

Oh, she'd thought she'd moved on, but one glimpse of Angus had shown her how untrue that was. She'd just moved.

As if moving would make a difference when what ailed her was inside her—when it came with her wherever she went, like an illness in remission.

So! The time had finally arrived when she had to put the past behind her once and for all.

Would talking to Angus help this process or should she phone him—tell him not to come?

Probably.

She dressed and walked up to the medical centre,

switching her mind from personal matters to medical ones, wondering just what the fallout of the lifting of the quarantine would be.

'We're all on telly,' Grace greeted her, waving her into an empty patient room where several staff members were peering at the small screen of a television set.

Beth recognised the mobile lab, sitting on the beach, and there was Grubby, walking around with his bag of dead birds. Then a still shot of someone in scrubs walking up the beach.

'Dr Angus Stuart, prominent epidemiologist, leaving the bio-hazard lab on Wallaby Island.'

'There were flashes of light last night—a photographer,' Beth muttered. 'The figure in white in the rainforest—he or she has been here for a couple of days. Who knows what photos we'll see?'

The news report showed more shots of the island, taken from a helicopter, zeroing in on the medical centre.

The next switch was one that surprised them all.

'That's Charles,' Grace whispered. 'And Jill and Lily when she was still in hospital—how did someone get that shot?'

It was definitely inside the hospital, but could have been taken through a window, and it showed two desperately anxious adults—parents? It certainly looked that way, with one of them on each side of a little girl lying still in a big hospital bed.

Beth was silently cursing the fact that she and Angus hadn't done more to find the figure in the bushes, or found someone to track him or her down, when Grace gave a hoot of laughter.

'Oh, look, there's you!'

Grace's comment diverted Beth and she looked at the screen again, then shook her head in disbelief. The sweet peas on her pyjamas had come out beautifully, as had Garf, but it was the condom drooping out of his mouth that caught the attention, and in case no one recognised it for what it was, the label of the well-known brand was clearly visible on the torn packet. There she stood, knee deep in the bushes, fighting an unlikely-looking dog for the wretched condoms, while a voice over prattled on about her being the doctor in charge of the medical centre.

'Oh, no!' she whispered, unable to believe this was happening. Even Grace had stopped laughing and was looking at her sympathetically. The impression given by the broadcast was that if this was the person in charge, no wonder there'd been an outbreak of bird flu, somehow insinuating further that by having such a person running the medical centre everyone on the island, including vulnerable children, would be put at risk. 'I can't believe it!'

'It doesn't mean anything,' Grace said, but Beth could hear the phone ringing in the office already and knew there'd be an avalanche of calls, not only from the press but from anxious parents.

Needing to escape, she went in to see Robbie, who was sitting up in bed, playing with a small hand-held computer game.

'Hey, Dr Beth, come and see my score. I beat my last one.'

Beth stared at him. Was this the child who'd been so sick? She went over to the bed and sat down to check his score, then asked him how he felt, although the question seemed unnecessary.

'I'm better, a bit tired, but can I go back to camp? Jack went back, and Lily.'

Beth checked his chart.

'Maybe later,' she told him, thinking of the times they thought he'd been recovering and then he'd relapsed. 'I'll come and see you after lunch.'

She wasn't on duty until that night but she checked on Susie—Alex and his daughter, Stella, were both in the room, one on each side of Susie's bed, each holding one of Susie's hands. Susie was going to be all right.

Beth closed the door, not wanting to intrude on what was obviously a private time for all three of them, and made her way to the office. Cal Jamieson was there.

'So, what's happening, apart from the doctor at the new medical centre appearing on TV in her pyjamas?'

Cal smiled at her.

'Quarantine's lifted. Mike's airlifting a lot of the Crocodile Creek staff back to the mainland today and I imagine the resort is putting on extra boat and helicopter trips to take their guests back. Luke's still rostered to be here this week with you—you're on tonight, aren't you?'

Beth eyed him doubtfully.

'If you still want me as the doctor here,' she muttered. 'The way the TV made me look, it might be easier to ride out the waves that follow the bird-flu scare with someone else in charge.'

Cal gave her a stern look.

'Do you think we haven't all been caught in our pyjamas, or in some equally embarrassing situation some time in our lives?' he said, then he smiled. 'Though I'd love to hear the story of the condoms some time.'

Beth felt a blush rising from her toes.

'I didn't want any of the kids walking past there and finding them in the bushes, then Garf came along and he thought it was a game,' she said, stumbling over the words in her haste to get them said.

'Of course,' Cal said, still smiling.

The door opened behind Beth, and Gina breezed in.

'Have you asked her about the condoms?' she demanded of her husband.

'Of course,' Cal told his wife. 'She didn't want any of the kids finding them in the morning.'

'Oh, really!' Gina's eyebrows rose but her smile was warm, and filled with fun. 'Poor you!' she said to Beth, giving her a big hug. 'If I were you, I'd go hide somewhere until tonight. The story will soon get stale, the press will vanish back to wherever they come from, and the island will return to normal.'

She released Beth, then added, 'And I just loved the pyjamas!'

Beth had to laugh, which was much better than wallowing in mortification.

She still had a job, and Gina was right—the press would go and the island would get back to normal.

Though it might never be the same again for her…

CHAPTER NINE

HIDING worked for Beth until lunchtime, when Sam came looking for her.

'I did catch a fish and it wasn't a king but an emperor, a red emperor. You have to come and look at it before Grubby and Bruce cut it up so we can have it for our dinner. Come on!'

He grabbed Beth's hand and led her towards the back of the dining room, Beth wondering just what Angus had meant by 'later' and whether, by going on this expedition to meet an emperor, she would miss him.

Which could well be for the best. After seeing herself on television that morning, all the great maturity she thought she'd managed to achieve seemed to have wilted, and she felt as raw and insecure as an intern.

'See!'

Grubby and Bruce were standing by the stainless-steel bench where fish were scaled and gutted. Beth had wondered whether small children needed to see this process but although most of the girls made noises of disgust, the boys seemed to love watching.

'Wow!' Beth said, for it was a truly wonderful fish. A

pinkish red, with a high snout—exactly the kind of snout an emperor should have. 'That's a great fish!' she told Sam. 'Did you take a picture of it?'

'Benita did and she sent it on her phone to my mum and dad and they texted back to say 'Wow' just like you did. Grubby's going to cut it up and I'm going to give a piece to Lily because fish is very good for getting better when you've been sick.'

'You'd better not leave it on the deck,' Beth said, thinking of the flower.

'Of course not, silly. Malcolm the cook will cook it 'specially for her, and he's going to cook some for me and some for Benita and some for all the other kids. Would you like some?'

Beth shook her head.

'No, you guys eat it,' she told him, 'but thank you for letting me look at it.'

'That's okay. I'm going to lunch now,' Sam told her, and with that he took off, busy as ever, a little boy packing a lifetime of experiences into every day.

Beth wandered back to her hut, not wanting to get into conversations about pyjamas or condoms with any of the staff or volunteers. She'd have a bowl of cereal for lunch, then catch up on some e-mails, maybe have a rest…

It all sounded good but as she climbed the shallow steps to her deck she knew she was returning to her cabin in case Angus came, stupid though that might be!

Immature as it undoubtedly was!

But she did do busy things, keeping herself occupied until mid-afternoon when she heard the noises of the camp children returning along the beach from an exploration of the coral reef that was visible at low tide. Wearing thick-soled sneakers, they were able to walk in the shallow pools and enjoy the sight of the bright coral polyps and vivid waving tendrils of the sea anemones, watching small fish darting around and molluscs moving across the sand in search of food.

She'd joined in the reef walks the previous week, marvelling at the life beneath the water. Now, peering out at where the little group chattered as they walked along the sand beside the translucent blue-green water of the lagoon, she was sorry she hadn't joined them, while the sounds of their talk and laughter reminded her of the joy inherent in this job, and she found herself relaxing for the first time that day.

So the scream didn't mean much at first. Kids often screamed—with laughter or pretend fear, or sometimes for no conceivable reason at all.

The second scream, though, was of pain and terror, and she took off, leaping her steps and racing to the beach, where she could see figures now huddled together.

'Get the kids back,' she said to Benita, who was kneeling on the sand beside a young boy—Sam! 'Do you know what happened?'

Benita shook her head.

'He just screamed and fell down,' Benita said, looking as puzzled as Beth felt.

'Take the other kids back to the camp and phone the medical centre—tell them to send the medical cart.'

Beth was holding Sam's wrist as she spoke, feeling the fast beat of his pulse, but his chest was barely moving. Respiratory arrest?

'I'll take his towel,' one of the children said, reaching for a bundled-up blue towel that had evidently fallen from Sam's hand.

Respiratory arrest!

'Don't touch it,' Beth snapped, bending her head to breathe air into Sam's lungs. 'Just go.'

She didn't want to panic the children and hoped the urgent look she gave Benita would tell her to hurry.

'Breathe, Sam,' she prayed, settling her knees more firmly on the sand, then pinching his nose and breathing into his mouth again, short sharp bursts of air, head turned as she breathed in so she could watch his chest move as she filled it for him. Expired air, not good enough, but all she could offer until the cart arrived with oxygen.

She counted and breathed and prayed they'd get there soon, counting, breathing, praying, warily eyeing the towel from time to time.

'Respiratory arrest?'

The voice broke her rhythm, then Angus was kneeling on the other side of Sam.

'I'll do the breaths, you take a rest,' he said. 'I saw the group near your hut. The emergency cart should be here before long.'

Beth sat back on her heels and watched Angus for a minute, then she looked around, seeking a stick of some kind—a lump of driftwood, though not, this time, to hit Angus with it! Saw a piece a few metres away and went to get it, then, using it, she unwrapped the towel.

'Damn!' she muttered, and as Angus raised his head momentarily, she pointed the stick at the shell.

'That's a cone shell,' a strange voice said, and Beth

turned to see a tanned man in faded shorts and little else standing behind her. 'Poisonous.'

But Beth had no time to be chatting to strangers, although he had confirmed her thoughts. She knelt beside Sam again, remembering where the towel had been lying near his hand, searching his skin for a break where venom might have been injected.

'Here!'

It was on his little finger, and she reached across and pulled a handkerchief out of Angus's pocket. Thank heavens he was a man of habit—of course there'd been one there!

She wrapped it tightly around the finger, and then the hand, not certain what good it would do but remembering, when she'd studied all the dangers on a coral reef, that pressure immobilisation of the affected part was recommended.

'Four hours!' she muttered to herself. 'Clinical recovery has been documented after four hours.'

Angus glanced up at her, but she didn't have her thoughts enough in order to explain to him.

Besides, his attention had to stay on Sam, and on breathing for him.

The cart arrived, and Luke jumped out. Beth used the stick to drag the towel, with the small, innocuous-looking shell on it, out of the way.

'He'll need to be bagged,' she said, as Luke set up the oxygen tank and mask. 'Assisted ventilation and a mild sedative—the pain must be what caused him to pass out, although not breathing wouldn't help.'

But as Luke slid a cannula into the back of Sam's hand

and prepared to give him the sedative, the little boy's eyes fluttered open.

'Hurts,' he said.

Beth held his bandaged hand.

'I know it does, sweetheart,' she whispered. 'But just lie still and Dr Luke will make that better soon.'

The eyelids drooped closed again and Beth looked around. Should they keep treating him here or transport him to the medical centre?

'Do you think he's stable enough to move?' Luke asked, putting her thoughts into words.

'Maybe stay here for a few more minutes,' she said. 'I'd like to see him breathing on his own but if he doesn't then we're better off in the medical centre, where he can go on a respirator.'

'Good thing we've taken Susie off it,' Luke said. 'What happened?'

Beth pointed to the shell on the towel, but although the towel remained, the shell had gone.

'Cone shell. It was wrapped in the towel. A man was here, he knew it was poisonous so I suppose he took it to dispose of it. I saw him pick it up so he knew how to handle it. He should be safe. I don't know them all by name but it looked like the geographus, which is the most poisonous.'

Luke looked surprised.

'I was coming to work on an island where these things live—of course I looked them up. Irukandji jellyfish, seasnake, stonefish and cone-shell envenomation just to name a few. That innocent-looking shell is a cone shell. They shoot out poison through a toothed harpoon in the narrow end of the shell. My guess is Sam picked it up at the fat end and, because all the kids know you're not to touch shells or plants or anything in the national park, he wrapped it in his towel to hide it. It stung him through the towel, which should have further minimised the amount of poison that got into his body, but he's small…'

She stopped talking and started shaking, thinking how close a call it was for the little boy she'd grown so fond of.

'He's breathing on his own,' Angus announced, and Beth looked down to see he was right. He'd stopped bagging and Sam's chest was rising and falling naturally.

'Let's get him up to the centre,' Luke suggested.

'Sit in the cart, Beth.' Angus kept his eyes on the child as he spoke. 'I'll pass him to you.'

Had Angus seen her shaking?

Not that it mattered. She climbed into the cart and watched as Angus lifted Sam gently and carefully, while Luke handled the oxygen bottle and kept the tube from kinking.

Angus bent to put Sam in her arms and their eyes met, so many memories flooding back, so much history, so much pain and sadness flashing between them.

She'd been mad to think they could go back—mad to think having an affair with Angus would give her special memories. More heartache, that's all it would have given her…

'The towel.'

Thank heavens Angus hadn't been distracted by a look between them.

'The towel…' She hesitated. 'I'm concerned about the towel. I don't know if the cone shell barbs detach, in which case one could be in the towel and still be potent.'

'I'll bag it and see it's destroyed,' Angus responded. 'There's a shop at the resort where we can buy Sam a new towel.'

We?

We sounded so good but Beth knew she shouldn't give it any special meaning. It was only a figure of speech. It probably included Luke as all three of them had worked together to save Sam.

But Angus *had* come over to the camp, presumably to see her—to talk…

She could feel the tremors she'd felt earlier returning, but they weren't relief this time.

Stupid thinking!

She held Sam carefully, talking to him, assuring him it would be all right, turning her thoughts resolutely away from Angus, thinking instead how weird it was that the scene that had played out only two days earlier with little Danny being driven up off the beach should be repeated.

Although Sam would be all right, she was sure of that.

Two hours later, feeling unutterably weary and with her shoulders tight from sunburn she'd suffered when she'd knelt on the beach, she made her way slowly back to her cabin.

Settling Sam into bed had taken far longer than she'd anticipated and although Luke was in charge, she had stayed with the little boy, knowing he trusted her and wanted her near. Wanted her to hear his story, how he'd picked up the shell so he could show it to Lily because she'd missed the walk.

Now, with the wound excised and dressed, and with a mild sedative dripping into his veins, Sam was sleeping and she was free—at least until eight when she was due on duty again.

Her cabin was in shadow, the sun already down below the mountain, but not so deep in shadow she didn't see the movement on her deck.

She stopped, remembering the intruder who'd photographed her the night before, but as the figure stood up, she realised it was Angus.

'I'm sorry, I thought you'd have gone back to the resort. I should have let you know I was delayed.'

'You shouldn't have done anything. I knew you'd want to see Sam settled. He's okay?'

Beth nodded, stopped now at the bottom of the steps, not wanting to go up them—to get close to Angus.

But she could hardly stand there for the next four hours and her shoulders were stinging. A hot shower might help.

She came up the steps into the light and heard his oath, looked at him, puzzled, but he wasn't looking at her face but at her shoulders.

'Oh, for heaven's sake, Beth, of all the harebrained ideas I've ever heard, someone with your fair skin coming to live on a tropical island must be one of the worst. Get into the shower, stand under cool water—not too cold, you could go into shock. I'm going over to the kitchen and I'll be right back.'

He strode away—long, angry strides.

So much for diamonds, Beth thought tiredly, unwinding her sarong as she made her way into the bathroom.

Where she saw what Angus had seen—bright red shoulders!

'Damn it all!' she muttered, then she sat down on the toilet seat and thought about having a really, really good cry.

The thought of Angus returning from the kitchen—why the kitchen?—and finding her with red eyes as well as red shoulders put paid to that idea, so she stood up again, started the shower, and did as he'd suggested—stood under lukewarm water, which felt so good she considered staying there.

Until she heard his footsteps on the deck and knew she didn't want to be naked when she saw him. Naked meant vulnerable—very vulnerable.

She dried herself, patting the red bits gently, then wrapped a clean sarong around her body and walked into the living room. Angus wasn't there. He was in the kitchen and, if she wasn't hallucinating, he was peeling cucumbers.

'Come in here and sit on the stool,' he ordered, his voice suggesting she'd better not argue with him right now. 'Let's try this.'

Totally bemused—by the cucumbers as well as this officious, bossy Angus—she went, and sat, then sighed with pleasure as cool inner flesh of the cucumber skin rested on her reddened shoulders.

'I have no idea if there are any scientific benefits in cucumber skin, but once when I was five we had a holiday at the beach and I got sunburnt and my mother put cucumber skin on it.'

Beth sat motionless beneath his ministering fingers. Even if she'd wanted to move, she doubted she could have, for in all the time she'd known him, Angus had never, ever, mentioned his mother.

Let alone suggested the family had ever done anything as ordinary as having a holiday at the beach.

'But as I was saying earlier, Beth, it really is the height of stupidity for someone with your fair skin to live in the tropics.'

He was back to scolding her, yet there was a note of something she couldn't quite put a finger on beneath the cross, hectoring tone.

Something soft—fond almost…

'And running away,' he continued. 'That doesn't solve anything. We both did it, I know that.'

He moved, taking fresh skins and putting them across her shoulders, flinging the used bits in the sink.

'Didn't talk. Stupid, really, because I knew where you were coming from with not talking—not about emotions—but with the way you were brought up, who could blame you? But me—well, you've met my father, know my upbringing. But you'd think intelligence should have made me realise how wrong he was.'

Angus's voice was softer now—far-away somehow—but nothing he was saying was making much sense, although Beth knew, deep down, it was important.

'You've never mentioned your mother before,' she ventured, and felt a piece of cucumber skin slide lower down her back.

Heard Angus sigh.

'Part of not talking,' he said gruffly, moving the skin across her skin, pressing coolness against the heat. 'They fought—that's my only memory of them together—raised voices, bitter with recriminations and hot with accusation and counter-accusation. One morning, I was seven…' His voice faltered and he held the cucumber firmly against Beth's shoulder as if needing to hold on to her right then. 'It was particularly bad. I stayed in my room until the last minute, thinking I could just dash out and up the road to school and not see either of them, but then my father left and as I headed for the door, I heard my mother crying in the kitchen.'

Beth held her breath, not daring to move, wanting so much to hear the rest of the story—wanting even more for Angus to tell her, to talk to her.

'I went in there and she tried to pretend she was all right, but her eyes were red and there were tears on her cheeks. I put my arms around her waist and told her I loved her, then I went to school.'

Long pause.

'When I came home she was gone. I never saw her again.'

Beth bent forward, holding her head in her hands—not crying, but in so much pain for Angus she could barely breathe. Then she stood up, forgetful of the cucumber skins, which cascaded to the floor around her, and moved towards the man who, pale and gaunt, faced her across the kitchen.

'Oh, Angus!' she whispered, and wrapped her arms around him, resting her head on his chest, feeling his hands tentatively settle on her waist. 'Oh, Angus!'

What else could she say?

How could she explain the pain she felt for the little boy he'd been and for the man he'd grown into—the one who dared not say 'I love you' for fear of losing the recipient of that endearment.

His chin rested on her head and she felt so comfortable

and at peace it took her a moment to realise he was talking again.

'It made me over-cautious about love, and as for expressing it—impossible! Then you were pregnant and we married and that's when I should have said it, but you'd never mentioned love and I figured if I said something, I might frighten you away. I was so happy, Beth, and it seemed to me that you were, too, even without words. But deep inside where betrayal lived I couldn't believe someone as alive and vibrant as you could love a dry, emotionless person like me. I had doubts…'

He paused again, but Beth knew there was more, and she stayed where she was, in Angus's arms, listening to him purge the past.

'That was weakness on my part—and further weakness when you went into labour. I hated the thought of seeing you in pain, scared the words I hadn't said to you would be torn from me, and I'd lose you, too. I let you down, not being there from the beginning at Bobby's birth, but I let myself down even more when I walked away from you after Bobby's death, burying myself in my work. When I didn't argue. When I told myself it was what you wanted—that I was doing it for you—but if I'd been half the man I should have been, I'd have fought, Beth. Fought for your love, fought to win it.'

The words brought not understanding but a thousand questions, and as comfortable as she was within the warm circle of his arms Beth had to move.

She pushed away and looked up into Angus's face.

'Did you just say that you loved me—back when Bobby was born?'

Angus nodded, a ghost of a smile on his lips.

'So much I was afraid I'd have to tell you when I saw you in pain—have to say the words that could send you away from me! But how could I not love you, Beth? You were light, and sunshine, and colour, and everything that was ever good that had happened in my life!'

Beth frowned at him. It sounded wonderful, but surely she was missing something here.

'You thought all that and didn't tell me?'

He nodded again, looking less hopeful now—the smile gone.

'And you still feel something for me? This scolding and the cucumbers—that was love?'

Definitely no smile now. In fact, he was looking distinctly uncomfortable.

'It's how I could show you my feelings. Talk is difficult—we'd established that.'

Beth waved away that pathetic excuse.

'Just tell me,' she said, folding her arms across her chest, needing to get everything out in the open.

He paused, moved his shoulders uneasily, then said, 'I love you, Beth.'

She smiled.

'No hug?'

Angus didn't move.

He couldn't.

Tension held him rooted to the kitchen floor, cucumber skins scattered around his feet. He looked at the woman—the second in his life to whom he'd said 'I love you'—and wondered just how big a mistake he'd made in saying it.

Was he too late?

Had there ever been a right time?

He waited until the waiting became impossible, then took a gamble.

'You're supposed to say it back,' he said, surprising himself at how firm and strong his voice sounded, considering the jelly-like mess he was inside.

'Nuh-uh!' his ex-wife said, shaking her head with a great deal of determination. Defying him, his usually biddable Beth! 'Not until there's a whole lot more talk going on. For instance, if, as you say now, you love me, why the business of not having an affair?'

'You should know that,' he said, recovering slightly, wondering if the slightly less reddened skin on her shoulders meant the cucumber had helped.

Ha! That was his mind escaping from the talk he found so difficult—science didn't need a lot of talk.

'Well, I don't,' she told him. 'It doesn't make sense to me at all.'

He took a deep breath, moved closer, put his hands on her waist and, holding her, looking down into her wide-open eyes, he tried to explain.

'What you were suggesting—an affair, holiday romance—that's not what I want with you, Beth.'

He felt the tremor that ran through her body and longed to draw her close, but drawing her close would lead to kissing and kissing would lead to bed, and that's how they'd got into this impossible situation, making love instead of talking, thinking their unspoken communication—body language in its truest form—was enough.

Beth waited, her body aching for closer contact, her head filled with rosy light. Angus loved her—but sex and rosy light weren't quite enough. More words had to be spoken—dragged out of him if necessary.

'What *do* you want, Angus?' she asked, then wondered if she'd gone too far—tempted fate just that fraction too much.

'I want you,' he said, his eyes holding hers, telling her things she'd never seen in them before. 'I want you in my life, for ever. I want to wake up in the morning with you in my bed, in my arms, and I want to go to bed at night with you beside me. I want you sharing all my joys and triumphs and my lows and disasters, and I want to share yours. I want to marry you and stay married to you for ever because without you my life is empty and meaningless.'

He kind of smiled, an expression so uncertain it tugged at something in Beth's chest, then he added, 'Will that do?'

Would it?

Not quite—in spite of the tugging.

'Not quite.'

She said the words this time and saw his startled reaction.

'Beth?'

Her name was a plea but she waited. He was intelligent, he should be able to work it out.

Except that this was all new territory for him, talking about emotions as foreign to him as Icelandic. In fact, knowing Angus, he probably knew some Icelandic.

'Don't you want to know how I feel?'

His face paled and his hands tightened on her waist, then dropped as he turned away.

'You don't love me? Of course, why should you, after the way I treated you, the way I wasn't there for you when you needed me, the way I walked away at the end? Of course! How stupid can a man be? Standing here babbling on about wanting you for ever, embarrassing you no end with all of it, expecting you to say you love me. I'm sorry, Beth.'

She caught his hand and pulled him back towards her, moving so she stood in front of him and now she put her hands on his waist.

'For such an intelligent man, Angus, you are incredibly stupid. Tell me something, why did we get married?'

'Because you were pregnant?'

'Exactly!'

'So, what are you getting at?'

'How do you think I felt?'

'About getting married?' Angus was guessing here, the conversation having gone far beyond his understanding, probably due to lack of practice in this type of conversation.

'Yes,' Beth confirmed, and Angus tried to think. They'd both been happy, he was sure of that. They'd found a marriage celebrant and asked her to marry them in the children's ward, Beth wanting the kids to share the event, he happy because it had been where they'd met.

'I don't know,' he finally admitted, wondering if he'd failed some test, although the vibes between them still seemed as strong as ever.

'I felt guilty, Angus,' Beth whispered. 'So guilty. As if I'd trapped you into something you didn't want—had never wanted. You were so complete in yourself, or so it seemed to me, that you didn't need anyone else. The only thing I could do, I thought back then, was not compound the problem by making silly declarations of love—declarations I was certain would be unwelcome to you.'

'You loved me then?' Angus asked, but even as the words came out he knew the answer. Of course she had, showing him in a hundred ways every day just how much she'd loved him, and he'd accepted it as Beth simply being Beth.

But that had been then and this Beth was someone he didn't entirely know or understand.

'And now?'

She smiled and he felt his heart stir in his chest, expanding to a point where he felt actual pain.

'Of course I love you, stupid. Always have and always will.'

He moved closer, enveloping her in his arms, wrapping her close to his body, finding her lips, kissing her, hands roaming over her satin-soft skin—

'Ow! My sunburn!'

He stepped away from her, searching through the strewn cucumber skins for an unused one.

Beth stopped him with a touch of her hand on his arm.

'I'm sure there's some cream at the medical centre that might work better than cucumber skins,' she said, then she smiled, 'And as the condoms ended up in the bin we may as well go up there and find it.'

He dropped the cucumber skin into the sink and took her hand, drawing her close and kissing her, not touching her sunburnt skin at all…

CHAPTER TEN

THE medical centre was quiet. The press who had come in with the lifting of the quarantine had lost interest when the story turned out to be about mosquitoes, not bird flu. Entomologists had also flown in, suggesting to the rangers that the mossies be controlled with sprays for the moment and people warned to wear repellent at all times.

Luke had discharged Robbie after lunch, and although Sam had been admitted for observation overnight, according to Marcia, who was the nurse on duty, he'd eaten a good dinner—a fillet from the fish he'd caught—and was now sleeping peacefully.

Ben and Mr Woods had both left that morning, but Susie remained, giving Beth, now sensibly clad in long shorts and a checked shirt, a total of two inpatients.

'Huge caseload!' Angus teased, as Beth led him into the small pharmacy.

'More like what I expected to have,' Beth told him. 'The medical centre is necessary as support for the camp, and the resort owners put in money as well, because they like to be able to assure their guests there are medical facilities close at hand. But no one ever foresaw anything like the panic that happened this week.'

'And now?' he said, repeating the question he'd asked earlier.

Beth had found the cream and Angus had pushed her shirt off her shoulders so he could rub it into her skin.

And now? she pondered as his fingers spread the cream, bringing relief to the still tingling burn.

'What do you want?' she asked, her nerves tensing as she realised that for all their talk nothing had been settled. Oh, they'd sorted out the past, but what of the future?

'I've told you what I want,' Angus replied. 'I want you, with me always. I realise you have a job here, and obligations, and I know you have to think about it—think about our future—but it's clear in my mind that I want us to be together—always.'

Beth turned to look at him, but he was concentrating on the tube of cream, carefully putting the cap back on it.

'Just the two of us?' she asked, forcing the words out through the tightness in her chest.

He looked up and half smiled.

'I'd like to have another child with you, or children, but that's up to you.'

He drew closer, touched her cheek.

'Another child wouldn't replace Bobby, not in my heart or mind, and not in yours, I'm sure. Another child would be just that—a person in his or her own right. But think about it, Beth, think what an opportunity it would be for you and me to have a child or children to whom we could give all the love we both missed out on in our childhoods. I sometimes wonder if it was partly that—our own childhoods—that made us love Bobby so much—and made his death so hard to bear.'

Beth rested against his chest and felt his arms enfold her, low down around her waist, pulling her close, holding her safe against his chest—against his heart, which he'd now pledged to her.

Another child?

A child to shower with love?

A child she didn't have to give back when camp finished?

Angus's child!

Or children…

'I was so afraid,' she whispered. 'It hurt so much when Bobby died, I didn't think I could ever live through that again. I didn't want to have to.'

Angus felt her anguish and held her closer.

'And now?'

It was becoming a refrain.

She eased far enough away to look up into his face.

'And now…' She smiled. 'With you beside me, loving me, I—'

'Hey! Oh, I'm sorry! Didn't know I was interrupting anything, but I was looking for you, Beth. Sam woke up, he wants the dog, and I wondered—'

Beth pushed away from Angus, heat in her cheeks rivalling her shoulders for redness.

'It's okay, Marcia. Angus was just putting cream on my sunburn.'

'Exactly!' Marcia said, grinning from ear to ear.

'But Garf!' Beth continued, hurrying her words to cover her embarrassment. 'I don't think we can have Garf in the medical centre.'

'Not Garf,' Marcia explained. 'The dog in the top hat you gave the camp kids. Sam says it will make him happy while he goes to sleep.'

Beth considered that, then shook her head.

'I don't think we can do that. If one child starts to take camp things to help him or her sleep then they'll all want to. I know he's in hospital but it sets a precedent. Oh, dear…'

'I think I've got an answer.'

Beth had been trying to forget that Angus was there, but his voice made her turn.

'An answer?'

He looked very uncomfortable.

'In my things,' he muttered. 'I've got a dog just like it. I could lend it to Sam overnight.'

His eyes met Beth's and she sensed his embarrassment, then he shook his head and shrugged his shoulders.

'You've got his little chair, I noticed,' he said defiantly, and she had to smile, although inside she felt like crying to think that all this time Angus had held on to Bobby's toy—not only held on to it but travelled with it so he, too, always had a little memory of his son.

'Tell Sam we'll be with him in a moment,' she told Marcia, and as the other woman walked away Beth turned back to her ex-husband and put her arms around him, drawing him close.

'Of course we'll have other children,' she whispered. 'We've far too much love to not be sharing it.'